The Tommy Good Story

"From Ashy

...To Nasty...

... To Classy"...

A Novel By:

Leondrei Prince

Street Knowledge Publishing LLC
Website: www.streetknowledgepublishing.com
Myspace: www.myspace.com/streetknowledgepublishing

The Tommy Good Story®

The Tommy Good Story

Published by: Street Knowledge Publishing
Written by: Leondrei Prince
Edited by: Dolly Lopez
Cover design by: Marion Designs/ www.mariondesigns.com
Photos by: Marion Designs

For information contact:
Street Knowledge Publishing
P.O. Box 345
Wilmington, DE 19801
E-mail: jj@streetknowledgepublishing.com
Website: www.streetknowledgepublishing.com
Myspace: www.myspace.com/streetknowledgepublishing

ISBN: 0-9799556-0-2
ISBN: 978-0-9799556-0-0

This Book Is Dedicated To:

My first and only true love... can you remember your first love? I remember everything about mines, from her falling arches, all the way to her swelling up when she ate certain stuff – mainly shrimp – but she was stubborn. She'd eat it anyway. I even remember our song; it was Prince's "Adore You." Life is crazy as hell, because you can't rewind the clock and no matter how much I want to I can't. The two of us have grown up, grown apart, and now have our own separate lives. I'm very happy for you and your marriage. You deserve to be happy! As for me, I'm still trying to find my "nitch" in life. I guess I can say I'm a late bloomer, and I'm just starting to blossom ☺. I do have one thing of yours though, that no one will ever be able to take from me and that's my memories of you...

Do you remember your first love? Well, I remember mines and it makes me smile to remember the first times...

...For my first love

Acknowledgements

First and foremost again I want to give all praise and thanks to Allah. Woke there continues to pick me up each and every time I fall down only to make me better than the last I fell... Allah-Akbar!!! (God's the Greatest!!) To my mother, Ms. Deborah Prince (may you rest in peace).

Now for my most important shouts... I first want to shout out myself because I don't give myself enough credit for the things I do. I battle the obstacles of life every day and still land on my feet. Leondrei, you dat nigga!! I want to shout out I my grandmother (Gammy) you're the best! My lil' brother and sister Radee and Rayya. No matter how grown y'all get y'all are still my babies – mommie said so!! To my best friend "Dee" – Da Mom - thanks for everything!!! Thanks for using your own judgment instead of the advice from the crabs. RIP Co-co – it was foul the way they did you man. To my nigga Stimey from 9th if it wasn't for you, on our ten year bid, I'd never finished one book – thank you man! To my baby Lynn Gist and my boy Ulysses Beard – Uncks "UL". To my boy, Xavier "Zob" Wilson sorry for forgetting you in the other books but you know how it goes... you save the best for last. Whass'up nigga!! To my cousin Snook and his wife Tia, whass'up y'all? "Dadda-boy" Whass'up baby!! To Da-daughters whass'up y'all? Y'all know who y'all are..."G.M.B." for life, Ha! Ha! Cousin Mike "Dog" Lindsey, Sponge, Cousin Cub – hold ya' head nigga. To Sara Bronson, I love you baby! To my baby Numbers and Jade... whass good y'all? To my sister Susie Cunningham, hey baby! Love ya! To 'da Bluff down in ATL. To my boy Manny – "Jig" Holla at me boy and hold ya head. The best thing you could have done was to get away from da crabs. To the boy Bruce Stewart, Tommy Good was inspired by you baby! Hold ya head, your legend lives! Last but not least to my brother, friend, cousin, and confidant, Art "Jamar" Lee (Easter), whass'up boy! Hey Tamiryah & Tameera, y'all know I could forget "the daughters". To my brothers from another mother: Mr. Dean Pritchett, Mr. Dwayne Washington, Mr. Omar Coverdale, Mr. Maurice Hunter,

iv

Lenny Brown, William Davis, Jermaine Dollard, Lionel Benson, Jermaine (Marlon) Wright, Michael (Mike Mike) Wright, Mr. Michael (Mujähid) Chambers, Kevin Chambers... my daughter, Ms. Khalia Thomas.

I want to thank all the distributors to carry my books. Special shout out to Hakim in Philly on Broad & Erie – Black & Noble Books – As Salaam Alaikum brotha - and Shakron for everything. I want to thank all the bookstores that carry my books especially Mejah Books in my home state of Delaware. Ninth Street book store too!! Khalil on 15th & Market, Philly, Pa.; Urban Anthony, Philly, Pa., my peoples, "Carvellos" the bookman, Washington, D.C. and Pretty Boy Books and distribution, Mr. Logan and Dontaé —one love!

I want to thank my cover designer Kenny (A6 Media). Y'all blazed the cover, thanks! I want to thank my boy JoeJoe for stepping into a new game with me – the book game – thanks, baby boy. I learned a lot from you. Good luck in all your endeavors. I want to thank my sista Mrs. KaShamba Williams for all of her advice and a new life in this book game, love ya!! I want to thank all my true fans for all the love and support! Whass'up Coast 2 Coast Bookclub... hey, Taraya – Baltimore's number one reader – whass'up girl? Hey Lady Scorpio, whass'up baby? Hey Diva's Dream Big book club. Thanks for the love!

To my fellow authors: Mr. Al-Saadiq Banks, Mr. Treasure E. Blue, Mr. Richard Jeanty, and the rest of y'all!

Chapter One

The Ashy Years
1986

The dilapidated three-story home on the east side of Wilmington City was where it began for Tommy Good. Living in a house that was packed to capacity by almost every relative in his family, Tommy found out early that the luxuries of the world were a long way from 809 Popular Street.

His mother, who was rarely around, left him and his lil' brother, Marcus, on their grandmother, "Big Mom", while she chased behind a no-good ass nigga named Lester.

Lester was an old-school player whose only real means of survival came by perpetrating the fraud and he was good at it. He dressed real nice, wore jewelry, drove a nice car *and* was always well mannered. Dude talked real intellectually all the time--talked so good that many overlooked that he really wasn't shit--except for Tommy. Lester played women for a living and Tommy's mother, Candice, was one of them. She was just too stupid or too love-struck to see the signs, but not Tommy. Tommy hated Lester, and hated his mother for being so naïve to the weak ass game Lester was running on her. Besides that, he loved his mom to death. That didn't stop him from doing all kinds of shit to break them up, but it never worked.

"Mom, where you going?" asked eight year old Tommy Good as he stood in the doorway in his favorite G.I. Joe pajama jumpsuit.

"Why? You ain't my daddy," she smiled at her firstborn through the mirror as she felt his protectiveness. "Besides, I'ma be alright."

"But I want you to stay home with me," he pleaded as he watched her put on her eyeliner and blush.

"Tomorrow, okay?" she answered, but she knew it was a lie. He probably wouldn't see her for the next two or three days.

After that came the knock on the downstairs door.

"Candice!" Big Mom yelled from the bottom of the stairs. "Lester down here, chile!"

"Okay, Mom. Tell'em here I come," she said and lit up like a Christmas tree.

Tommy just glared. He turned away from the door in disgust at how she could just smile and glow whenever that dude's name was mentioned, but yet she'd looked at him and Marcus, her own sons, like they were sore thumbs. This made Tommy stomp down the stairs.

"Boy, whass your damn problem?" Big Mom asked as he stormed into the living room, nearly tripping over Lester's alligator shoes. "I know you better say excuse me!" Big Mom demanded.

"X-cuse me!" Tommy spat, and sat down on the couch next to Big Mom with his arms folded across his chest.

"Lester, I'm sorry, baby. Sometimes this boy gets a little besides himself. I don't know what be getting into him," Big Mom apologized for Tommy's rudeness, then popped him on the thigh.

"What'chu do 'dat for?" he stared, rubbing the sting away.

"No need to apologize, Ms. Good. I understand quite well why he's mad tonight," Lester smiled, then, chuckled under his breath. *That lil' nigga betta go the fuck 'head,* he thought to himself, and smiled when Candice appeared. *Mmm, mmm, mmm! Look at this bitch!* he said to himself, nearly slobbering out of his mouth.

Candice was twenty-four years old--sixteen years his youth, young and naïve. She thought she recognized game from all angles; truth was she didn't know cornbread from pound cake, or greens from spinach. Her two older sisters, Rhonda and Robin, who lived in one of the six rooms with their kids, would just shake their heads at her sillyness, while her baby brother, six years younger than her, Bearacus (a.k.a. Bear), would scold her all the time because they were the closest of her siblings.

"I told you to stop fuckin' wit' dat lame ass nigga! That nigga is a fake pimp, and I think dat nigga gettin' high!" Bear swore by his words.

"Everybody get high," Candice replied in his defense.

"Everybody don't smoke no mu'fuckin' crack!"

"He don't smoke no crack!" she snapped.

"He do too!"

"How da fuck you know?"

"'Cause, you dumb bitch, I sell crack!" Bear was trying to tell her without really putting it out there, but Candice's love-struck ass was taking a long time to catch on.

"You ever sell him some?"

"No, but I sold a muthafucka some who was driving dat nigga's Volvo, and he said it was for his boy, 'Les', not knowing that I was your brother."

"Well, Les was probably gonna sell it."

"Not no got-damn dime he only paid seven dollars for!" he said, and gave her a look like, *now what?*

Regardless, she thought as she looked at her Lester. *This is my man and he can do what he wants,* she told herself, and headed straight into the comfort zone of his strong arms.

""Hey, baby," he charmed, then kissed her softly on the mouth.

"Hey, honey!" she responded, only to hear from her son.

"Get off my Mommy, punk!"

"What'chu just say?" Candice scolded him with anger in her voice.

"Baby, don't worry about it," Lester charmed, trying to get her out the house.

"Don't tell me that, Lester. This is my child. Now, what'chu say?" she snapped, getting closer to him.

"I ain't say nuffin," he lied to her, which made Candice kick off her shoe and wear his ass out. *"Whack! Smack! Bap! Whack!"* the shoe sounded as Tommy danced trying to escape the blows. He did so much jumping and bouncing around that Bear came running up the steps from the basement.

"Damn, Candy! That's enough! Why you keep beatin' the boy all da damn time? That's why he's always snappin', 'cause all you do is beat him. Damn! Spend some time wit' da boy instead of spending it wit' dat crack-head ass nigga!"

Candice couldn't believe he said that shit, and not in front of Big Mom at that. "Why you tellin' dem lies in front of Mommy, boy?" she defended Lester once more.

"Man, I ain't lying. Dat nigga smoke crack," he said, staring Lester in the eye.

Lester wanted to say something back to the young boy named Bear, but he knew better. People in the street didn't call him Bear for nothing. At 18 years old, Bear was a beast, towering over nearly every average man at 6' 4½". The ones he didn't, he outweighed, tipping the scales at a solid 265 lbs., all muscle. So instead he said, "Baby, I'll be out in the car."

"Okay," she said, and looked to Tommy who started the whole mess.

"It ain't his fault he know dat nigga ain't right," Bear said, defending his nephew. "Come on, Tommy. You comin' downstairs wit' me. You want to sleep downstairs wit' me tonight?"

Tommy hurried off with his uncle.

Candice stormed out of the house, but before she shut the door she screamed at Tommy, "When I get back I'ma tear dat ass up again!"

Chapter Two

Uncle Bearacus -- "Bear"

"**D**on't worry about your mom. I ain't gonna let her beat you," Uncle Bear assured his favorite nephew as he carried him on his back down the hallway to his basement door and opened it up. "Watch your head," he said as he headed down the stairs.

Tommy loved his Uncle Bear more than anyone in the world. He admired him so much that even at 8 years old he tried to walk, talk and act like his Uncle Bear. As they neared the bottom of the steps, Tommy smelled the ever so sweet smell of those little joints he called "reefer" and heard the sweet sounds of Prince's song, *Adore You* playing through the speakers and he knew his uncle had company.

"Until the end of time, I'll be there for you... You are my heart and I truly adore you..." Mia sang along with Prince, not hearing Bear and Tommy come downstairs. "Oh shit!" she said startled. "Baby, you scared the shit outta me!" she finished, popping up from underneath the covers butt-naked.

Tommy covered his eyes. It was the first time he'd ever seen titties other than his mom's or Big Mom's, and neither one of theirs looked like Mia's. Mia was as pretty to Tommy as the picture of Mona Lisa was to artists and scholars, even though he was eight years old. He knew what pretty was, and Mia was that and more. Her skin wasn't light, and it wasn't dark either. It almost looked olive, like maybe she was Hawaiian or from the island of Trinidad. Her body was perfect in all aspects of standards, and her eyes were the color of a Siamese cat's -- that goldish color with black pupils. They almost looked haunting, but they weren't. They were drawing, almost hypnotic, and that's why they were so unique. The more Tommy thought about the woman who was

6

beyond his covered up eyes, the more he felt his "Little Peter" getting hard.

"You wasn't scared. You just ain't want me to hear you singing, that's all," Bear said, and pointed to Tommy. "Look," he said under his breath and pointed down to Tommy's little hard dick and smiled. "At least we don't gotta worry about this lil' nigga growing up and being no punk," he whispered.

"Aww, ain't dat cute," Mia blushed, and told Bear to uncover his face.

"Boy, why you got your face covered. What? You ain't never seen no titties before? I know damn well you seen your grandmom's."

Tommy embarrassingly laughed at his uncle.

"The way she like to sleep ass naked," Bear said about his mother.

"But I ain't never seen no real girl's before," Tommy said honestly, and Bear knew what he meant.

"Well, it's alright, Nephew, 'cause you can get a good look at those. Do you want to touch 'em?" Bear asked, knowing he would be scared to, but their surprise, Tommy said, "Yeah!"

"Go ahead then, nigga," Bear encouraged him and watched as his nephew climbed up on the bed and crawled over to Mia. *That's my lil' nigga!* Bear thought to himself as he watched his nephew play with Mia's titties. She just smiled.

For the rest of the night Tommy was in La-La Land in the comfortable presence of his Uncle Bear and had totally forgotten about he way his mother made him feel hours ago.

"I love you, Uncle Bear," Tommy said before going to sleep.

"I love you too, lil' nigga," he said.

■■■■■■

When Tommy woke up the next morning, it took him a minute for his eyes to adjust to his surroundings. Then he remembered he wasn't in his room -- he was downstairs in Bear's domain. He sat up in the bed between his uncle and Mia and climbed out the bed. He stood on the side of the bed and stretched, then realized why his mom cut the feet out of his favorite sleeper. It was too small.

Tommy could hear all the footsteps upstairs and he knew that everyone was awake, and by the smell of things, about to eat breakfast if they hadn't already, so he decided to get up there before everything was gone.

When he stepped from beyond the opened basement door, he bumped right into his Aunt Rhonda. Rhonda was his two cousins', Ronett and Theresa's mom.

"Boy, watch where the hell you're going! And go wash your damn face and brush your teeth," she said, and kept moving.

"Where my mom?" he asked his Aunt Robin, as she stood in front of the stove.

"I don't know where she at, baby. She ain't come home last night. Are you hungry? You want something to eat?" she asked, and he responded with a nod of the head.

Like his Uncle Bear, Aunt Robin was his favorite aunt. She was the eldest of Big Mom's kids, the one who held the family together, and she was Kendra and Kenny's mom, his two eldest cousins. He got along with Kendra but Kenny was a bully. He couldn't wait until he got older so he could whip his ass. With that thought still fresh on his mind, he bumped right into Kenny who was in the living room watching wrestling, and Tommy knew it was about to start.

"Whass'up punk?" Kenny said, and stood to his feet, "Come on, let's wrestle. I'll be Superfly Jimmy Snuka and you be Special Delivery S.D. Jones."

"I don't want to wrestle," Tommy told his big cousin, who was three years older than he was and much larger than him in size.

"Yes you do, now shut up!" he said and put Tommy in a headlock.

Kenny slung him to the floor and jumped on his back and pulled Tommy's head up by the chin like the Iron Sheik used to do, and Tommy started to cry. Then, from out of nowhere Ronett smacked the life out of Kenny.

"Get off him, punk! Now wrestle me like that. You always picking on somebody smaller than you," she said, and commenced to whipping his ass in the middle of the living room floor.

"Y'all cut dat shit out!" Big Mom snapped. "Rhonda and Robin! Come get y'alls' kids! I'll be so damn glad when y'all get da hell outta my house, I don't know what to do!"

"I know, Mom," Willie, her eldest son said as he awoke to the commotion. Big Mom had a large family, three daughters and two sons.

"That goes for yo' ass too! Thirty got-damn-somethin' years old still livin' home wit' cha mom... You oughta be shamed of yo'self!"

"Shit, Robin older than me!" he said, not getting the point.

"But Robin has an excuse, and will be gone as soon as her divorce settles." She looked Willie up and down waiting for him to respond to that.

"Dat's right, nigga! Gone as soon as I get my money. I can't wait either. Especially to get away from your always drunk, stinkin' ass feet having self. I see why Cathy don't want yo' ass! Who wants a dirty nigga!" Robin said as she came from the kitchen.

"Fuck you!"

"Yeah, dat's all you can say about me, nigga."

"Y'all stop dat shit in front of these kids," Big Mom said as all of her grandchildren looked on.

"Come on kids, let's go eat," Robin said, and they all went and sat around the kitchen table.

It would be days like this that Tommy would remember the most when he got older. And he'd remember what life was really about as he'd flip through old photo albums. Right now though, he dreaded these days because there was never enough money, never enough clothes, never enough love or affection, and most of all, never enough attention. Life was fucked up being a "never enough" type of nigga.

■■■■■■

Uncle Bear came up from the basement followed closely by Mia and shook his head in disgust. There were just too many people living under one roof. *I'ma 'bout to move up outta here,* he thought to himself and walked over to the kitchen table. "Gimme some," he said to Tommy, and picked up his plate, wolfing down two huge fork fulls of his eggs.

"Boy, why is you eatin' up all dat boy's food?" Robin asked. "Here, it's some left over here."

"I'm cool."

"You want some Mia?"

"Nah, I'm straight. We about to go to breakfast now."

"Yeah, come on Tommy. You want to go wit' us?" he asked, starting a whole bunch of *"I want to go!"* chants from all his nieces and nephews. "I asked Tommy, not y'all," he told them. "Come on, boy. Go put some clothes on."

When Tommy came back downstairs Bear snapped. He was tired of holding it back any longer; he had to say something about the way Tommy was looking.

"Yo! Why Candice be lettin'em dress like dat? Look at his sneaks and shit," Bear said, and Robin agreed. "I know. That's fucked up!"

"She probably giving dat nigga all her money or either she gettin' high wit' dat nigga," he finished.

"I don't know why. She lettin' 'dat nigga bring her down," Robin concluded.

"It look like she getting skinny too, don't it?"

"Bear, you know you tellin' the truth now!" Robin agreed.

"Fuck it! If that bitch wanna be stupid, let her. But I ain't gonna let them suffer. I'ma go buy him and lil' Marcus some sneaks and shit."

"That's a bet, 'cause I was about to do something too," Robin said seriously.

"Well, don't worry about it 'cause I got 'em now," Bear said. "Come on, Tommy. We outta here."

And that's just how Uncle Bear was. He wouldn't let anything happen to Tommy or the rest of his nieces and nephews because he was different. He saw it in Tommy's eyes. Tommy was different. He was special. He had the sure fire in his eyes as did Bear, and Bear quickly acknowledged that.

Chapter Three

Tommy's New Best Friend

"**A**www man! Why you gotta park this big dumb truck right here?" Tommy whined, as the huge U-Haul truck parked right in front of the telephone pole that they had hammered a crate to and played basketball on.

"They must be moving in right there," Ronett said.

"I hope they got some kids," Theresa said.

"I know, 'cause we need some new friends. I'm tired of playing with Sharon and them. They always starting sumptin', then we wind up kickin' they asses," Ronett spoke truthfully like she was grown.

"You better stop cussin' 'fore I tell Aunt Rhonda," Kenny said.

"And if you do I'ma whoop yo' punk ass again," she assured him.

Tommy sat on the edge of the curb with his arms folded and basketball between his feet and watched as the lady climbed down from the truck. She stood there in the street with the door open and waited for her kids to climb down before she made another move. Tommy looked at the boy and girl who seemed to be his age and Kendra's, and noticed that the new kids looked just alike.

"Are y'all twins?" Ronett yelled from the steps before anyone else could.

"Yes, they're twins," the lady said.

"I told y'all," Ronett bragged as she confirmed his suspicions.

"Do y'all need some help?" Tommy asked, standing up and walking across the street.

"I don't know. Let me ask my husband. Michael! Do we need any help?" she asked the big burly man in her deep southern accent as he rumbled around in the back of the truck.

"Yeah! They can help with some of these damn boxes if they want to," a voice echoed through the truck.

"Why y'all talk so funny?" Tommy questioned.

"We don't talk funny… you do," the boy and the girl snickered at him.

"Whass yo' name, handsome?" the kind southern woman directed her attention to Tommy.

"My name is Tommy."

"Well, Tommy, my name is Mrs. Patricia, but Mrs. Pat is fine. These are the twins, Michael and Michele, and that's my husband, Mr. Michael." She smiled with two teeth trimmed in gold.

"You can call me Mike," Lil' Michael butted in.

Tommy smiled back at Mrs. Pat and laughed at how she pronounced "husband". He instantly felt connected to them, even gladly introducing his cousins to them.

"Where y'all from, sounding all country?" Kenny blurted out.

"From Decatur, Georgia," Mike puffed up with a deeper southern accent than his mom's.

"Is that the country or sumptin'? 'Cause y'all talk like them people in old slave movies. And most of them were from the country somewhere," Theresa asked. She talked so fast they barely understood her question.

"No, but everybody from the South has an accent," Michele said innocently.

"Oh," Theresa responded, and they commenced to helping them move into their new house.

From that day forward, Michael and Michele made lifetime friends.

■■■■■■

Tommy was up bright and early as usual. Getting up off the couch he slept on, he walked upstairs and barged into his mother's room. However, she still wasn't home. It had been almost a week since he last saw her and he began to cry. *Why my mom don't love us no more?* he asked himself without having the answer. He was worried about his mom and he missed her. All he could think was that it was Lester's fault.

Tommy had cried his last tear that morning. He refused to shed another tear for his mother or anyone else. Crying made him sad and depressed, and he didn't like it. He put on his new clothes Uncle Bear got him, put on his new sneaks and took his bike outside to go check for his new friend, Mike.

"Mrs. Pat, can Mike come outside to play?"

"Come in, suga. I'll get Michael." She turned away with her long housecoat and a tight apron tied around her waist. "Tommy, we're about to eat breakfast in a little while. Would you like to eat with us?"

"Sure!"

■■■■■■

After they ate breakfast, Tommy and Mike rode their bikes around the neighborhood with Tommy leading the way. They rode in the middle of the street, which Mike wasn't accustomed to, but he did it anyway.

"This is where they be selling drugs…" eight year old Tommy guided him. "…and right there, that's a crackhouse," he laughed pointing, but only for a second because right after the laughter, sorrow took control of his emotions. His world was crushed.

Candice came walking out of the same crackhouse wide eyed as an owl frantically looking in all directions. She looked a hot mess with the same clothes she had on the last time she left the house. Tommy couldn't believe his eyes.

"Is that what a person looks like on crack?" Mike innocently asked with his face torn up. "Because that lady looks dirty; she looks like she stank."

Tommy couldn't speak. When he found his voice to reply, he turned to him and said, "Come on, let's go!" But his move was too slow because his mom spotted him.

"*Tommy!*"

"Tommy, that lady is calling your name!" Mike was startled.

16

Tommy stared blankly.

"Tommy, I know you hear me calling you!" Candice yelled again with crusted lips.

"Tommy, dat lady is callin' you!"

"Come on, Mike, just come on!" Tommy hastily peddled on his bike while Mike tried to catch up to him.

Tommy was so hurt inside that it felt like his heart was about to bust. His nose was heavy and it felt like he was on the verge of sneezing, but he knew it was from holding back his tears. Seeing his mother walk out of that crackhouse had hurt him like he'd never been hurt before, but he wouldn't cry. He couldn't cry, because then he'd be a liar. He vowed to himself that he'd never shed another tear, and he was sticking to it. Deep in thought about what happened, he didn't realize that he was peddling at top speed leaving Mike behind.

"Yo, Tommy!" Mike called out to him, "Wait up, I'm not from 'round here!"

He slowed down for Mike to catch up. "My fault."

When Mike finally caught up to him, he had a strange puzzled look on his face.

"Why'd you take off like that?"

It was tough but Tommy decided to tell him the truth instead of having to explain it later when he was sure that Mike would see his mom sooner or later. So he said, "If I tell you sumptin', you gotta promise not to ever say anything to anybody, okay?" He stopped peddling and began to walk with his bike by his side.

"I promise," Mike answered and began walking along side of Tommy.

"That was my mom," he mumbled ashamed, and dropped his head down. Mike was speechless. He didn't know what to do or say, because he'd never seen or knew anybody who smoked crack, so he didn't know the effects of what the drugs did to a person. The only thing he did know was that Tommy was really humiliated.

"Your mom? Why she smokin' crack? I heard that's really, really bad."

"Me too. I don't know why she doin' that." Tommy rubbed his nose and snorted the snot.

"Well, why are you so sad? It's not you smokin' crack, so don't feel bad." That was the best Mike could think of saying, but it worked. Tommy felt a little better. Not because of what Mike said, but because even though his mother smoked crack it didn't change their friendship. He was still Tommy's friend and showed him by giving him a hug.

"Sometimes, a hug can make you feel better. That's how us folk do down South when sumptin' wrong. Now, I hope you feel a little better."

"I sure do," Tommy said as he embraced him.

Chapter Four

Addiction Is A Mothafucka!

Candice put the powder on the tablespoon, took a pinch of baking soda from the box and let a few drops of water drip onto the spoon. She watched as it bubbled up, then held a lighter underneath the spoon and began to cook the cocaine. Just the sight of the coke cooking and turning into an oil right before her eyes made her stomach bubble for the drug. It was crazy because for the first time in her life, Candice was powerless over her body and mind. The drug controlled her now. She thought about her sons, Tommy and Lil' Marcus. She remembered her conversation with her brother, Bear, and how he warned her about Lester smoking crack, but she didn't want to believe it, not even after the first time she smoked it with him. Now she had been hooked and couldn't stop.

As she slowly cooked the rock on the spoon, she flashed back to the night she left home like it was yesterday, which in reality was a week ago.

This is so fucked up! she reminded herself, as the innocent and naïve Candice left her body for good that night. She knew Lester was getting high when Bear told her. She'd known this and got high with him the second week she was involved with him. But she didn't understand why Lester would be so stupid to have someone cop from her brother like he wouldn't find out.

"What are you about to do?" Candice asked as they sat in the living room of Lester's condo.

"I'm about to take me a blast, baby."

"A blast? What's that?"

"I'm about to smoke me a rock."

Candice frowned up her face. "A rock? A crack rock?"

"Yeah, a crack rock. Why? You want some?"

"Hell to the naw! I don't want none of dat shit! Are you crazy? How can you fix ya' mouth to ask me to smoke some damn crack?" she said angrily.

"Why you say it like that? You act like sumptin' wrong wit' it. I don't say shit when you smokin' your weed and shit."

"Lester, that is weed; It's not crack!"

"Ain't nothin' wrong wit' smokin' crack. It's only sumptin' wrong wit' it when you let it get out of control."

"Well, maybe it ain't catch up to you yet 'cause all the mothafuckas I know that smoke it are fucked up."

"Candice, look around you, girl. Am I fucked up?" he tried to convince her placing the rock in his homemade crackpipe, the one he made out of a miniature Jack Daniels bottle and a glass stem with Brillo stuck in the tip of it.

"No, but..."

"But *what?* I'm straight." From the looks of things, Candice couldn't deny the facts. Lester was slim but muscled and still handsome. His spot was laid. Everything from the welcome doormat to the dirty clothes hamper was new and up to date. So she let it go. *Maybe he's right,* she thought, and watched as he prepared to smoke his rock.

20

Lester grabbed the piece of broken hanger and tied a piece of cotton to the tip of it. He dipped the homemade swab into a cap full of grain alcohol and lit the tip with a lighter. Candice watched intensely as he moved the flame up and down the glass stem and smoke filled the bottle. If only she would have followed her own intuition instead of the lead of her man.

"Here, you try it and tell me if it's that bad."

Candice hesitantly paused.

"Hurry up now for all the smoke goes out!"

She slowly reached out and placed her mouth on the little Jack Daniels bottle, sucked in her cheeks and inhaled. Instantly she felt better than weed could ever make her feel. Now, here she was addicted -- smokin' ninety going north trying to get high again.

She dropped a few cold drops of water onto the spoon she held and used her index finger to mix the stuff. The once oily substance began to get hard and form into a rock on her fingertip. Using her thumbnail, she plucked the rock onto the tabletop and broke a piece off.

"Here, Lester," she said, and slid the piece across the table to him.

Like Lester, Candice learned how to work her light up and down the glass stem until the smoke of the drug filled her lungs. She grabbed her chest and held her pipe tightly in her hand as the high began to kick in. Candice backed up against the door and nervously let her eyes roam around the living room.

"You hear that?" she asked Lester in a delusional state of mind, but Lester ignored her. "You hear that shit?" she frantically asked again, yet he didn't respond.

Cocaine has a way of making you believe you are hearing things, or that people are watching you, putting you in a paranoid state.

After the initial shock of the drug wore off, she began to calm down. Then the reality of what she had done all week long began to flash through her mind like nightmares, especially the most degrading thing she'd ever done in her life.

Candice and Lester had smoked the last of the 8-ball of cocaine together and were flat broke and fiending for another hit. Lester and Candice rode over to the east side to a crack house and parked out front. He told Candice to hold on while he went inside to see if he could get some credit from the old man known as "Pops". He was sure Pops would give him credit because he dealt with him many times, but this time Pops said "No".

"What'chu mean no, Pops?" Lester couldn't understand why the old fat man who smelled of musk was denying him credit as good as a customer he'd been.

"Just what I said, Les. You still owe me money from last week."

"I told you I'll pay you on Friday. Just add it to my bill. My woman get her welfare check that day, so you know I'm good."

"Where your woman at now?" Pop asked, scratching his potbelly.

"She out in the car."

"Which one is it? That pretty young thang from 'round the corner? Uhhh, what's his name's sister -- Bear?"

"Yeah, it's her. Why?"

"'Cause you might not need no money."

"What'chu mean?"

"I mean if you can get her to you know... Uh... do a lil' sumptin', then I got you," he smiled.

"I don't know, man. She might not do no shit like that." Lester was skeptical as he looked at the nasty rolls of fat. He couldn't picture Candice saying yes. Then he couldn't put it past her because he'd seen in his time of using, people do some nasty, degrading things to get high.

"Well, it looks like I ain't got nothin' for you," Pops toyed with him, flashing the bags of crack on the table.

"Alright man, let me go check."

Lester walked back out to the car with his head down, trying to come up with a way to ask Candice to do something with Pops so they can continue to smoke, but nothing seemed logical. Candice was one of the best he'd ever had and he damn sure didn't want to sacrifice her, but the addiction was overpowering. He tried to shake it but it wouldn't leave. The desire to smoke was just too strong. *Fuck it!* he told himself. *I'ma ask her.* He pressed his luck.

Candice saw him coming, but from the looks of things it didn't look too good.

"*Damn!*" she muttered, flustered at the point of no return and ready to go all out. In fact, she had already gone all out when she pawned her ring. The only thing left to do was turn a trick. She had seen women doing it all week long as her and Lester bounced from house to house, but she couldn't see herself doing it. However, now as she sat, broke, busted and disgusted, the only thing that would make her feel better was another hit; so the thought had crossed her mind. She wanted to bring it up to Lester a couple of nights ago before she pawned her ring but she hadn't hit rock bottom yet. But she was soon to see it... she was there now.

"What happened?"

"He said nah, he ain't got no credit."

"So what we goin' to do?"

"I don't know."

"Damn! Why he ain't giving you credit?"

"'Cause I still owe him thirty dollars. But he did say... never mind," he stopped before he stooped so low to ask her.

"Say what?"

"Nothin'."

"Nothin', what?" She was really getting antsy.

"He said he would look out for us if I could talk you into doing something with him."

"Like what?"

"You know, trickin'," the words left his mouth.

Candice knew he was about to say that and still, up to that very moment, she didn't understand why she didn't have the willpower to say no. Even the thought of this made her sick to her stomach.

Pops had seen them come in and was surprised when Lester told him it was okay. Candice couldn't believe she was actually about to disgrace herself as she looked at the old fart with a dirty black face.

His clothes were dingy like he had them on for days and his skin looked sticky from sweat. When he smiled, his rotten teeth were yellow, and from where she stood, it looked like he had a mouth full of Captain Crunch cereal.

"Com'ere," Lester eyed her up and down. And as she got closer to him he smelled horrible! The combination of sweat, lack of deodorant and not bathing had him smelling like a zoo animal.

Candice followed Pops upstairs into one of the rooms in the back. When they got in there, he cut on the light and pulled her close to him. He began to feel all over her body; the feeling was sickening to her.

"Can you please turn the lights back off?" she asked demandingly, not wanting to see what she was about to do.

She stood at the foot of the bed and listened to him get undressed as he breathed heavily.

"I'm ready," he said.

From this occurrence, Candice would never be the same. The shame she felt as she dropped her clothes, then dropped to her knees and performed oral sex on this fat, *nasty* stinkin' ass man would scar her for life. The thought of her doing this upset her stomach as she went up and down on his uncircumcised little penis. *I need some fresh air,* she gagged and stepped out of the crackhouse… and right in front of her was her son Tommy.

"*Tommy!*" she called out, but he peddled away.

■■■■■■

25

Bear was just leaving the block and heading home to count his money when he saw Tommy chillin' on the corner with Mike. He was just going to blow the horn and see his nephew when he got home, but Tommy flagged him down. Bear pulled his candy apple red 740i Volvo with the gold rag and deep ditch hammers over to the curb and waited for his nephew to approach the car.

"Oh snap, folk! That car is fresh to def!" Mike admired. "Who dat?"

"That's my Uncle Bear."

"Dat's ya' uncle?"

"Yeah, that's my uncle."

"Man, is he rich?"

"I think so," Tommy answered as he approached the car.

"Whass'up, nephew?"

"I know where my mom is."

"Where dat that heifer?"

"Around the corner at the crackhouse."

"What crackhouse? Show me." Bear exited his vehicle. Tommy and Mike's legs again peddled their bikes, and Bear followed them on foot as they headed towards the crackhouse.

"It's right there, Uncle Bear," Tommy pointed, and Bear knew exactly whose crackhouse it was. It was freak ass, old man Pops house.

"Ok Tommy. You and Mike go on 'round the house. I'll meet y'all there. Go now!" he demanded and they peddled off.

I'ma fuck this nigga up! Bear said silently. *And whoever else up in this muthafucka!* He knocked on the door so hard that they thought it was the police. *"Open this muthafuckin' door!"* he snapped, and Pops pulled it open. Bear busted straight into the house, shoving Pops to the side. "Get the fuck outta the way 'fore I fuck you up!" No one in the house moved. "Candice!" he called out. "Where's my fuckin' sista, nigga!" he growled, and punched some man in the mouth as he stood wide-eyed. "Where da fuck is she?"

"She's back there, man! Don't put your hands on me no mo'. I didn't make her come here! It was her old man, not me," he pleaded.

When Bear got out into the kitchen, he caught Lester and Candice trying to get out the backdoor. The sight of his sister looking the way she did filled him with rage as he angrily clenched his huge hands into fists. He was so fuckin' angry with her. She looked like each and every crackhead he served cocaine to daily. She looked no different. Her hair was going every which-a-way, her clothes looked worn and her eyes told it all. She had become addicted to the same shit he made his living from.

Bear was irate and the rage that filled his heart had made him blind with hatred. He charged at Lester as soon as he came through the room. After he whipped his ass real good, he pulled out his 45 from his waistline and put two bullets in him.

"I bet' not never see you 'round my sista again, pussy!" Bear threatened, and decided not to take his life. "And Candice, from here on out I'm not gon' let you take my nephew through this shit! I got my own place now and he's moving in with me and Mia."

27

When it was all over, Lester lay beaten to a bloody pulp and had to be escorted to the hospital by ambulance. No one said a word to the police about the incident when they arrived.

Chapter Five

The Summer They'd Never Forget

♫ *Nineteen eighty nine!* ♫

♪ *The number,* ♪

♫ *Another summer,* ♪

♫ *Get down!* ♫

♪ *Sound of the funky drummer!* ♫

"Fight The Power"

Public Enemy, 1989

Three and a half years had passed since 1986 and it was Tommy's 12th birthday. Uncle Bear had the street blocked off for a block party he was throwing for his nephew, and D.J. Mix was spinning the hottest records of the summer on his twelve-hundreds. Chuck D of Public Enemy was yelling *"Fight the power!"* in a time where youthful teens were recognizing the Red, Black and Green, while crack was slowly enveloping the community, and Uncle Bear was *that* nigga!

Tommy knew there was something special about his uncle because of the status he held throughout the community. And he kinda had it all figured out, but Bear did a good job at concealing things from him. He would find out what it was sooner than he expected, but for now it was his birthday party.

Like every year, Tommy's birthday indicated the summer. This would be the summer that would change the lives of him and Michael forever. The event that would take place would have an affect on everybody in the community, but it would delete a piece of Michael that could never be replaced. The only good that would come out of it all was that it would bring Tommy and him closer than anyone could imagine. They had become one mind, one body and one soul -- almost literally.

The entire block, from 8th and Popular to 9th, had been blocked off by cones and rope to prevent any cars from entering or exiting. Almost every kid in the neighborhood was in attendance. Uncle Bear, for the last three years after taking responsibility of raising Tommy, always came back to Big Mom's house to throw it up way big for his nephew's birthday. And this year was no different. There was plenty of food, music, and for the adults, plenty of grown folk goodies -- beer and good "green".

Tommy's appearance had changed. He was getting older. This year he sported a 'Philly' round haircut with a real deep shape-up. It was so deep it looked like the barber had drew it onto his outline. He had a gold nugget stud in his left earlobe and a gold nugget chain with his name "Tommy" on it. His maturing body was dressed in the flyest M.C.M. sweatsuit you've ever seen, with a pair of all white Adidas Forums.

"Yo, Tommy! You see dat girl right there?" Mike whispered.

"Which one?"

"The one right there with your cousin, Ronett, and the girl Latoya. I think it's her cousin."

"Yeah, I see her. Why?"

"'Cause she been staring at you all day."

Tommy stood on Big Mom's step and nonchalantly gazed over across the street to where his cousin Ronett, her friend Latoya, and the most beautiful girl he'd ever seen, stood. There was only one person in the whole world Tommy imagined that was even close to looking like the girl across the street, and that was Mia. Mia, Uncle Bear's main girl, was the only one in his eyes that could even stand next to the girl across the street. But still, the comparison was none. He tried his best not to stare at her but she was staring at him. He could feel her eyes on him. It was easy to make eye contact. His heart skipped a beat.

"Look at her," Latoya nudged Ronett. "My cousin is sprung!" she teased, but her cousin didn't hear her. She was too busy staring at Tommy.

"What'chu mean *sprung*?" Ronett giggled.

"Look at how she staring at Tommy."

Ronett had witnessed this recently since Tommy started to fill out. Almost all the girls blushed when they were around the handsome maturing chocolate drop. She even caught Latoya staring at Tommy before.

"Girl, everybody be staring at my lil' cousin like dat," Ronett announced proudly. "My lil' cousin is da shit!"

Davita, aka Vita, stared at Tommy with butterflies tingling in her stomach. *Oh, my God!* she thought as her thirteen-year-old hormones kicked into overdrive. *He noticed me!* Truth was, all the boys at the party noticed her. For one, she was the prettiest thing out there; and for two, she was a new face -- fresh meat.

Davita was Latoya's younger cousin from Washington, D.C. She had come to spend the summer with her Aunt Cookie and Aunt Sandy while her mother ironed out her differences in D.C. At first Davita didn't want to come to Delaware because her big brother, Sinqué wasn't coming. But when she got around her cousins she began to feel good about leaving D.C. for once. It gave her time to relax and actually see how another city put it down.

Delaware was much smaller, but the city of Wilmington where Davita came to visit wasn't slow either.

"Damn, Vita! Snap back!" Latoya spat into her cousin's ear, and snapped her fingers.

"Huh?" Davita responded, half hearing her.

"I said 'snap back'!"

"Oh!" Vita laughed. "My bad, Jo. It's just that that boy right there is *mmm, mmm, mmm!*"

"*Jo?* Why you keep callin' me Jo? And I heard you was hot in da ass!"

"What'chu mean 'hot-in-da-ass'! Girl, I'm thirteen and still a virgin. I never even kissed a boy. Can you say either of the two? I thought not. Aunt Sandy told my mom all about you and some boy named Brian getting caught doin' it, and you were only my age then. Now you fifteen, so whose really *hot in da ass*? And, I called you 'Jo' 'cause that's what we say down D.C. Get used to it, '*Jo*'!"

"*Ooooh*, girl, who caught y'all?" Ronett covered her mouth.

"My mom, girl," Latoya replied.

"*Oooooh*, that's crazy! Did she snap?"

"*Did she snap?* Girl, she beat me *and* him."

Ronett bent over laughing her ass off at her friend's stupidity. All she could think of was cool ass B getting his ass beat.

"So, like I said Jo... who's really hot-in-da-ass?" Davita repeated, using her D.C. slang. (Jo was a word or name that applied to anyone who was being talked to. It was equal to saying, "*Whass'up cousin?*")

"Vita, what? You like my lil' cousin, Tommy?" Ronett wanted to know because she could make that happen easily.

"That's your cousin, Ronett?"

"Yeah, girl. My favorite cousin too."

"No he ain't," Latoya jumped in.

"It is too. What? You want me to go get him or sumptin'?"

"No! Oh, my God, no! Don't go get him," Davita was nerve struck. She didn't know what to say if he came over to them.

"Why? You like him, don't you?"

"Yeah."

"Well, let me go get him then. How you gonna hook up with him if you scared to talk to him?"

"Okay. Go ask him if he wants to dance with me."

"I got'chu," Ronett said and switched away.

Davita's heart was beating faster and faster the closer Ronett got to Tommy. She really did like him and wanted to dance, but what if he said "no"? Just the thought of him saying that made her want to call Ronett back, but she was already talking to him.

"Tommy, Latoya's cousin said whass'up. Can she get a dance or what?" Ronett said, pointing to Davita and Latoya.

"Who?"

"Vita, the one right there," she pointed at her, and Tommy was hesitant. Not because he didn't want to, but because she was so pretty that he was nervous. "Boy, I know you ain't scared! Not Tommy!" Ronett instigated.

"I know, man. Go 'head and dance with her, folk," Mike said, excited for his boy.

"Ai'ight, ai'ight. Come on, Ronett. Walk with me over there,"

Tommy played it cool. He followed Ronett across the street towards Vita. Little did Vita know his heart was pounding harder than hers was. He walked up to the girl and almost couldn't speak. She was even more beautiful up close. Tommy let his eyes rest on her feet.

Davita was dressed in burgundy, mustard and black-colored plaid Gap shorts and mustard T-shirt that complimented her shorts. Her hair was done into a ponytail with a bang covering her forehead. But what got him was the Etienne Aigner sandals, the ones that slid on like flip-flops but had the leather strap that went around the big toe and the thick strap that went in between the big toe, and a thick strap that went across the top of the foot.

"Whass up?" Tommy asked nervously.

"Hi, " she shyly replied. "Happy birthday."

"How you know it's my birthday?'"

"Uh, this is your party right?" Davita smiled exposing her pretty teeth. "I'm Vita."

"I'm that boy, Tommy," he returned the introduction. "Would you like to dance?"

"Yeah."

Tommy led her out to the middle of the street, barely moving, just stepping to the music. It was as if D.J. Mix had read their minds and everybody else's mind at the party, because he felt the energy dying down. He grabbed a record he was sure to get the party back jumping. He flipped the record in his hand, dropped it down on the turntables and began mixing, scratching and blending the songs in. The street instantly became packed with kids, teens and even adults all ready to shake their asses, as Rob Base began, *I wanna rock right now!*

Mix saved the day as *It Takes Two* blasted through the speakers. Tommy snapped. He broke down all the latest dances and danced out the entire party. When he realized Davita couldn't keep up with him, he slowed it down a little bit, but she was still impressed.

Tommy can dance his ass off! she thought, and was glad she accepted his invitation to dance, because every girl there wanted to be where she was at right now. It appeared that way from all of the smirking stares she received as she danced with him. That didn't stop her though. Davita danced, danced and danced some more with the birthday boy, admiring him from head to toe.

After the D.J. played the dopest selections he could think of, from Stetasonic's *Sally Walk* to Big Daddy Kane's *I Get Raw*, all the way down to Rakim's *Microphone Fiend*, he decided to slow it down. Besides, the street lights had come on, the lightning bugs had became visible and the people started to clean up. So Mix said over the microphone:

"This is the last dance of the night. Let's give the last shout out to birthday boy, Tommy and the beautiful young lady he's been dancing with all day! We wish you many more, playboy!"

Mix spun the last record, as Keith Sweat's *Make It Last Forever* came through the speakers.

Tommy was *the shit* that night!

He was so far into Davita that it was just like only the two of them were there. Mike was a few feet away grinding up on some girl named Ann, who would later in life become his wife.

Tommy got up close to Davita and put his hands on her hips. Before he knew it, Davita's arms were around his neck and his hands were palming her butt as they grinded to the music.

"Let me tell ya, boy/ I really need ya Ba-a-a-by/Ba-a-a-by, Ba-a-a-by/ I can make it alright," she sang her version with her face buried into Tommy's neck and shoulder.

"You can't dance that good, but you sure can sing," Tommy teased, and she backed up away from him and playfully looked him in the eyes and said, "Who said you can dance?"

They shared a laugh.

Damn, how I wish I could make this last forever, Tommy thought. Both of them shared the same thought and embraced each other.

When the party was over, Tommy walked Davita around the corner to Latoya's house in Compton Housing Complex and sat on the front step with her. They laughed, talked and shared their stories. They didn't realize how late it was until Davita's Aunt Sandy (Latoya's mom), opened the door and said it was time to come in.

"Okay, Aunt Sandy," she acknowledged and Sandy shut the door giving her niece time to say good-night. "Well, I gotta go now Tommy."

"Alright, then I guess I'll see you tomorrow," he said, and there was an awkward silence.

"Alright," she replied, and it felt as if time had stood still. "Well?" She waited for a kiss, but he didn't catch it.

"Well what?" he asked, and she made her move.

Davita stood up, grabbing Tommy by the arms to pull him up with her and they stood face to face. She placed his hands on her hips and scooted up to him so close that they breathed each other's breath. Then she leaned in to kiss him. Neither one knew what they were doing; they were just copying off of what they'd seen. It was the first kiss for the both of them, one, that both would remember. Not because it was the best, but because of Aunt Sandy who caught them and screamed, *"What da hell y'all doin'!"*

The way they jumped made her laugh herself.

"Nothing," they both lied.

"Get yo' ass in here, Vita! And Tommy, go on home! Before I call Big Mom on your hot tail!"

"Okay," he hurried away.

■■■■■■

Things were as normal as they could be. The teens were having the summer of their lives. Michael and Michele ("The Twins", as they were labeled) were so close to Tommy that when they were introduced to other people, they were introduced as cousins.

The remainder of the summer, Tommy, Mike, Kenny and lil' Marcus went to Brown's Boys Club during the day, while Ronett, Theresa, Michele, Kendra, Latoya and Davita went to the Girls Club on 26th Street. Every day, after they came back to the neighborhood from the Boys & Girls club, they met on the front steps of Big Mom's house and enjoyed the evening until the street lights came on. Big Mom's house was like headquarters for them and the rest of the children in the neighborhood. It had been that way since Rhonda, Robin, Bear, Candice and Willie were their age. They were known for having such fun together that all the kids came to 8th and Popular Street to play in the streets.

The most popular game for the boys was two-hand touch football or basketball, while the girls played double-dutch or played in each other's hair testing out new hairstyles. When they played together, the most popular game amongst them was "the boys chase the girls" (or "hide-n-go-get-it" as it was better known). Sometimes they played "hot belt" or "relievio", but mostly "hide-n-go-get-it" was the jump-off. And that's what they were playing on this night. It was like a ritual for Tommy to chase Davita, Mike to chase Ann, cool ass B to chase Latoya, and the brothers, Leonard and Darnell to chase Ronett and Theresa. The majority of the time, Kendra and Michele just ran and hid for nothing. The boys had gotten tired of chasing them after numerous times of rejections, slaps in the back, pinches and bites, instead of some soft hugs and clothes rubbing, or luckily, a French kiss.

While the kids played their usual sports, at the playground in the park on 7th Street, and the schoolyard at Bancroft

Elementary School not too far from Big Mom's, Deacon Matthew Johnson, a well respected man of the cloth and a pillar in the community, would go undetected, lurking in the shadows of the night. He did this often as they played, wondering if he could get away with the evil that occupied his mind. He watched them hump each other and rub clothes, bringing him to an erection. Unknowing to all except for himself, Deacon Johnson was a sick man. He was sick and aware of his sickness. That's why he would pray for hours on end for God to save him and rescue him from the demons inside -- all the while, leading his congregation.

Tonight the evils were too much to overcome. He couldn't hold back any longer as he stood in the darkness and masturbated. He watched all the couples pair off to their own little private spots as they stayed out past curfew, waiting for his opportunity to strike. Then the moment came.

Kendra and Michele ran fast as they could as the two boys chased behind them. Kendra ran straight, and Michele turned the corner, but both boys chased after Kendra.

"That was a close one!" Michele said excitedly to herself as she hid next to the dumpster on the side of the school. She squatted down in the corner, pulled her knees into her chest and hugged them, hoping not to be found by anyone until the game was over.

Deacon Johnson watched intensely as she sat alone. There was no way her innocent twelve year old frail body could defend herself against him. Deacon Johnson was a huge man, twice the size of your average city worker, and strong. He stepped from around the corner in all black and looked like a shadow in the darkness.

Michele thought she heard something moving and got scared. It had become too quiet for her, so she stood up. There it was again -- the sound. Only this time it identified itself as footsteps. She darted out from behind the dumpster and ran right into the arms of Deacon Johnson.

"Shhh!" Deacon Johnson gestured, and wrapped one of his huge, calloused hands across her mouth. Michele kicked and screamed at the top of her lungs, but Deacon Johnson's huge hand smothered her voice.

"God, please forgive me!" The deacon prayed, but he knew he'd never be forgiven. That's because he wasn't all there anymore, and he hadn't been since Pastor Shepard took away his innocent manhood. He had hurt the young Matthew Johnson and scarred him for life. From that very moment, the moment Pastor Shepard told Matthew to pull up his pants and never say a word, he had never been the same person.

He turned to the Lord out of fear and guilt for what happened to him. He prayed for help for what he was capable of doing to someone else, and it worked for a long time. However, as this little girl kicked, screamed and cried for the Deacon's mercy, he knew he'd burn in eternal hell, just as he knew what Pastor Shepard was doing.

Deacon Johnson smacked Michele. He smacked her so hard and viciously with his other hand it almost knocked her unconscious. He dragged her back into the same corner behind the dumpster and brutally raped and sodomized her until her blood painted the ground where he laid on top of her and tore her apart. He cried as he thrust into her tiny body, but shook with pleasure at the same time. She was his fourth victim. When Deacon Johnson was finished with Michele, he beat, stomped and strangled her to death before tossing her into the Dumpster and leaving the scene.

"Please Father, forgive me!"

■■■■■■

40

The game had come to an abrupt end when cool ass B's mom called him to come in the house

"Brian!" she called from the balcony of the Compton Apartments. "Get cho ass in here! *Now!"*

When they heard the voice, everybody came from out of their prospective hiding spots and gathered in the center of 7th Street Park and said their good-byes.

Everyone seemed to have been having a good time. And they were, until they heard Brian's mother calling him. Her call sent off alarm to each and every one of them because it was way past dusk outside. It was dark. No one realized how late it was until they heard the voice. Then they panicked, all of them thinking the same thing: *I hope I don't get in trouble!*

"Alright, y'all. See y'all tomorrow." Brian walked toward his building.

"Okay." Latoya giggled.

"I told you I could catch you."

"I let you catch me, boy!"

"We'll see tomorrow."

"Whatever. Bye, Brian," she squealed.

"See ya, Latoya."

The teens headed to Compton Townhouse first because they walked Latoya and Davita home before going to 8th Street.

"Where's Michele?" Kendra asked when she noticed her friend's absence from the group.

41

"Wasn't she with you?" Ronett was sure she was.

"She was, but when we got chased we ran our separate ways."

"Well which way did you run?" Mike was concerned about his twin.

"I ran straight."

"Well where did she run?" Tommy anxiously blurted, and Kendra pointed in the direction of the school.

"She probably still around there hiding," Mike said, and they all headed in the direction of the school.

"*Michele!*" they called out, but she didn't answer. They listened, only to be answered by morbid silence. Mike began to feel worried, like something was wrong.

"*Michele!*" They called again.

Then Ronett stopped dead in her tracks.

"What's wrong, Ronett?" Theresa asked her sister, but she was too shocked to answer.

"What is it?" Tommy stopped and looked in the direction Ronett was looking in. When he saw it, he froze. It was only Michele's sneaker, but seeing it next to the dumpster was eerie. Mike saw it too. It was the longest walk he ever had to make, but Tommy made it with him. He'd never forget it.

As they neared the dumpster their worst fears were confirmed with every step of the way, as torn pieces of Michele's clothes laid tossed around the ground. Tommy and Mike walked closer together. When they reached the dumpster and looked inside, the memory of Michele laying there naked with one sneaker on, covered in trash and bloody from the waist down, would haunt them for years to come.

Mike reached inside and pulled his twin from the debris and watched as spaghetti noodles, old salad and pudding dripped from her lifeless body. When the other kids saw Mike pull his sister from the dumpster they screamed and ran off, leaving him and Tommy standing alone.

Mike looked up to his friend helplessly, but there was nothing Tommy could do. His other half was gone. He'd never be the same again because there would always be that emptiness he'd feel from losing his twin. It was true what they say about twins feeling one another's pain, because during that very moment he wished it was him lying there. His tears would fall forever.

Chapter Six

Life Goes On

The death of Michele sent shock waves through the entire community. People were afraid to let their kids go outside to play. They started locking their doors and windows -- something they'd never had to do -- and they'd even came up with a neighborhood watch program. Michele was the fourth victim that died the exact same way. This was the first time it occurred on the Eastside of town, making it a wakeup call to the community.

The police had no suspects and it started an outburst of complaints throughout the Black community.

"I bet if it was some lil' white girl, they would have found a suspect!" a woman shouted at a rally soon after Michele's death.

But it was like their cries went unheard. Most of the people blamed it on the crack cocaine that was flooding the communities, but the police didn't think so. They had a serial rapist/killer on their hands and they knew it.

There was a massive turnout for Michele's funeral. Florists donated tons of flowers. It was a real sad sight to see, but it was reality – a child tragically murdered. Michele's death would be remembered forever.

Tommy never left Mike's side. He had become Mike's shadow for the past few days, and his presence was more than needed. Tommy even went down to Decatur, Georgia with Mike's family for a second funeral for Michele so she could be buried with other family members at a local cemetery near her birth place. It was the longest week long process of their lives, but they made it through. Tommy and Mike's bond had become as strong as Teflon.

When they came back home to Delaware it was nearing the end of summer and everyone was trying to prepare mentally for school, which started in a couple of weeks.

Michael missed his sister Michele dearly, but realized that life must go on. So he kind of closed her off in his mind. He locked her death and the memory of it in a far away place in the back of his mind and threw away the key, but not without a sacrifice. That sacrifice would cost him a piece of his sanity.

For the rest of the summer Tommy watched as his friend started changing. It was like he was going crazy...like he didn't have a heart or something, because he became deadly. He started killing cats, dogs, birds, and any living creature he could kill except, for people. What Michael didn't know was that all this killing was a training ground for him later on in life. With every living creature that he killed the colder he became. When Tommy asked him why he was doing so much killing, Mike would just smile a sinister smile at Tommy through those faint eyes, and it would send a chill up Tommy's spine.

■■■■■■

Davita thought of every possible solution she could come up with to try and persuade her mother to let her stay with her Aunt for the school year, but she denied them all. Her reply was, "You live in D.C. with me, not Delaware."

"But Mom, Aunt Sandy said I could stay and so did Aunt Cookie."

"What I say?"

"But Mom..."

"*But Mom*, shit! You're bringing your ass home with me and your brother."

45

"When?"

"We'll be there tomorrow," she said, and hung up.

Davita looked at Latoya, and started to cry.

"God! She make me sick," she blurted, and Latoya already knew the answer -- Aunt Marsha said she couldn't stay.

Davita tried to look on the bright side of things, but thoughts of Tommy wouldn't allow her to. Yeah, she did miss her friends and her own bedroom, but it was all worth the sacrifice for Tommy. Her entire summer was like a fantasy. She felt like Cinderella of the ghetto and the clock had just struck twelve. The only difference, her carriage was still a carriage -- she just got snatched away from it.

"Where is he?" Davita asked out loud as she put her last suitcase in the trunk. "I told him last night that my mom was going to be here early."

"Girl, chill out! He'll be here," Latoya guaranteed.

"He need to hurry up," Davita said, then heard the words she dreaded hearing.

"Come on, child, I'm ready to go!" her mother yelled from downstairs. Davita was devastated. She took as long as she could coming down the steps, stalling for time, but he hadn't come. He had let her down and she became discouraged.

Bump him! she said to herself, and headed out the door with her mom.

"See you, Aunt Sandy! Love you, Aunt Cookie! And bye, Latoya! "Davita said out the window as she strapped on her seat belt.

46

"See you, Vita! Call me when you get home."

"Okay," she said.

"See you girls. Call us."

"Bye, Aunt Marsha."

"Alright y'all, and thanks again, Sandy."

"What are sisters for?"

"I heard that! Bye, Toya baby!" Marsha said, and they pulled off. "Why your face all tore up?"

"It ain't."

"It's probably that lil' boy you was kissing." But Davita didn't answer. "Hmm, mmmm! You ain't think I knew about dat one, huh!" And Davita smiled. "I knew that's what it was from," her mother said turning the corner.

Then she saw him. She turned around in her seat, sitting on her knees and waved frantically as Tommy ran behind the car, then she blew him a kiss.

"*Bye, Tommy!*" she yelled as loud as she could.

"*Bye, Vita. I'ma miss you, girl!*" Tommy yelled back running as fast as he could behind the car.

Her mother smiled as she watched the little guy run behind the car through her rearview mirror and reminisced on her first love. *Damn, them were the good ole days!* she remembered and headed South.

Tommy and Davita were heart broken.

Chapter Seven

The Introduction to Uncle Bear's Life 1992

♫ *I started small time/ dope game* ♫
♫ *Cocaine...* ♪
♪ *Pushin' rocks on the block I'm never* ♫
♫ *Broke man* ♪

Scarface – Ghetto Boys

Scarface of the "Ghetto Boys" had taken the rap world by storm with his ghetto take of a ruthless hustler turned kingpin. The O.G. from the 5th Ward Texas had planted the seed in every street corner hustler in the games' head that they could do the same. The result: more money, more homicide, and Bear was at the top of the game.

Tommy had just turned fifteen years old, growing up with an OG, making him feel more like brothers than uncle and nephew, and that's how Bear carried it. He treated Tommy like a little brother as he got older. Big Mom kept lil' Marcus. Tommy was hardheaded, always getting into to shit. Whereas lil' Marcus adhered to everything an adult told him. Tommy needed tough love and Uncle Bear taught Tommy everything he knew about life -- everything except what he did for a living. He didn't want Tommy to get caught up in his world, but he knew it was inevitable. Tommy would question him all the time about his lifestyle, but Bear would brush him off with, *"How was school today? Do you like high school? You meetin' the girls?"*

Tommy knew that he hustled, but wanted him to tell him because he also had an interest in becoming a hustler. It was in the

48

cards. Everything Bear had required money, and for him not to have a job, he had plenty of it.

The house they lived in was like no other Tommy had seen in his life. They had a two-story single home with a two-car garage and everything you could imagine on the inside of it. The house was peach and cream in color, lined with brass end tables, lamps, and mirrors. The couches and chairs were cream in color, along with the walls, while the rugs, blinds, and drapes were peach. It gave the house a look of elegance. It wasn't a soft look, it was smooth. The house looked like money, and so did every room in it.

Uncle Bear would always say to Tommy, "I don't care if Mike comes over here and y'all got some girls wit'chall, that's cool. In fact, I don't care I don't care how many girls y'all bring up in here. Just don't bring no niggaz up in this house!" he would repeatedly stress, and Tommy knew why. There was way too much expensive stuff in the house to take a chance on some nigga trying to steal it or come back and burglarize it. Bear was well-respected, but there was always an asshole out of the bunch who was willing to take their chances.

■■■■■■

Tommy and Mike had got out of school early because it was a half of a day, and Bear had forgotten all about it as he sat comfortably at the kitchen table breaking down the two bricks of crack cocaine he just got from his connect. Like clockwork, Bear would re-up every nine days because his clientele demanded so, and like every time he did re-up, he hated the part he was doing now, bagging up the shit. It was nerve wracking trying to stuff the little capsules with the rock, but it had to be done -- plus, the profit was pleasurable.

Bear spent $19,800 a brick, which broke down to $550 an ounce. He could have easily sold the ounces at $800 profit, but why, when he could bag it all up. That's exactly why he did it that way. Off of every ounce, Bear bagged up 25 bundles of caps, which was 20 caps a bundle. He sold each bundle for $50, which totaled $1,250, so after selling the kilo of cocaine, instead of having a $9,000 profit. he made a $25,000 profit. But the game would change later on in the years. That's why whoever the smart ones were back then, they were the ones still paid today, because the "cap" days of hustling were the sweetest days ever in the drug game.

Bear heard the keys go into the door lock but he didn't move from his seat or try to conceal what he was doing because he thought it was Mia coming in. *About time!* he thought, because Mia always helped him with the bagging. But it wasn't her -- it was Tommy and Mike.

"*Damn!*" Bear was temporarily immobile as he stood from his seat trying to find something to throw over the table. "Tommy!" he called, "You and Mike, don't come in the kitchen!"

Tommy heard what his uncle said loud and clear, but he went there anyway just to see what he was doing for himself. "What'chu say?" Tommy asked, peeking his head around the corner.

"You heard what I said, boy!" Bear snapped.

"Oh, my fault, Unc," Tommy replied and pulled his head back, but only after he got an eyeful.

"Your fault, huh?" Bear said flatly.

He done seen it now. I might as well tell him what I do, Bear contemplated and walked out into the living room. "Yo, y'all two com'ere," Bear began, and sat down on the loveseat across from the couch. "Sit down," he advised them and they flopped down on the couch eagerly anticipating the conversation about to take place. *Let me see where do I begin?* he asked himself the question.

"Alright, look: I know y'all done seen the coke on the table, so it ain't no need for me to be frontin' like y'all didn't. Tommy, I know you been wondering what I do, but you and Mike already know. I know someone in the neighborhood done told y'all sumptin', so I'ma bout to keep it real with y'all.

Look, I sell drugs. I've been selling for years. I sold drugs way back when we lived at Big Mom's house, Tommy. It's what I do," he paused to catch his breath, "...but it's not what I want for you, or you. I want better for y'all, feel me? I treat both of y'all as if y'all were my sons. I try to make sure y'all have everything y'all need 'cause I want' y'all to be happy. If you're not happy with who you are, you become someone else.

"For instance, like me: When I was y'all's age and living at Big Mom's house, I ain't had shit, because Big Mom had to raise all of us by herself. And since I ain't have shit, I wasn't happy. When I was in high school, I ain't have no gear, I couldn't pull no bitches, I was the broke dude. So what I do? I went out and got my own like Maddy Stone. I quit regular school and signed up for da "School of Hard Knocks". But y'all don't have to do dat shit. I keep y'all fly, y'all got girls, so it really ain't no need for y'all to step out of y'all element. Because once you step outside and create a false persona of who you are, you become that lie you've created. It's hard to go back to who you really are. Do you understand what I'm try'na to say?"

He gave them a life lesson, and Tommy and Mike nodded their heads that they understood.

Bear continued, "Listen y'all, I'm tellin' y'all these things because it's real. Why do you think I go to night school? Why do you think I stress to y'all to stay in school and get dat piece of paper? I do it because y'all can't do shit wit'out an education. Like I said, be who you are. We weren't raised to sell drugs, pimp bitches, get high, stick mu'fuckas up or none of dat dumb shit we do. But we do it anyway, and those are the things that take us out

51

of our element. 'Cause we tryn'a live up to this false image, feel me? Shit, so now y'all know what I do and why I do it," he finished, and they all turned their attention to the door as Mia walked in.

"Hey y'all, whass'up?" she asked in her normal ginger tone.

"Hey, baby," Bear warmly greeted her as she made her way to give him a kiss.

"I ain't interrupting nothin' am I?"

"Nah, you straight. I ain't talkin' 'bout nothin' you don't know. I'm just tellin' them some shit about life, and why I do what I do."

"You told him?" She knew the time would come sooner or later for Bear to tell Tommy about this side of him.

"Yeah, I told him."

■■■■■■

After Bear finished giving them their lecture on the how's and why's of the game, it was time to teach them the ropes.

"I don't want y'all to do this, but it's up to y'all. Tommy I've been seeing the hunger in your eyes. Now, I'ma ask you this only one time… you want to get involved in this shit?"

Tommy quickly nodded, "Yes."

Bear sighed loudly and cursed, "Damn! As he accepted the responsibility to school his nephew and friend on the do's and don't's of the drug game. Out of all of the years he hustled, this was the hardest decision he had to make to teach him the game, but he knew better than some Jo-blow's nickel and dime watered down teachings.

He took them into the kitchen and explained to them every gram, ounce and pound of the chunky white substance, along with its pieces. They were amazed at the numbers Uncle Bear was throwing around so freely, and it only enticed them to want the game even more.

"Listen," Bear warned. "Hustling is not a real job or an honest way of living. There are repercussions to this shit. You can get locked up, robbed, or killed over this bullshit. On some real though, hustlin' is good to know in case you get in a bind. Yeah, that's it. That's what hustlin's for. It's to get you out of a bind," he reasoned, more to himself, as he taught them how to cap up rocks to sell.

■■■■■■

The next day after school, Uncle Bear told them to meet him on 9th and Bennett Street. He said he was going to be at a crackhouse in the middle of the block, so he wouldn't be hard to find. Tommy's heart picked up its beat, and so did Mike's as they walked on the block Uncle Bear had forbidden them to come on until today.

They had rode past here on their bikes and shit like that, but as far as being out right defiant to Uncle Bear's orders, they knew better than that. So of course they didn't come down there to hang. They knew what went down on Bennett Street. That's how they knew he was a drug dealer. Plus the car he drove gave him away -- not the Volvo, the new 740i BMW. Bear had the flyest car in the city. In 1992, he drove like he was a lawyer, judge or a professional athlete, but he was none of the above.

"Boy, what'chu doin' down here?" a familiar voice called out, causing Tommy and Mike both to turn around.

"None of your business," Tommy stated flatly.

"Boy, who you talkin' to? I'm still your momma!" Candice responded like only a mother could, but it didn't matter. Tommy had lost respect for her a long time ago.

"You ain't my mu'fuckin' mom. You don't do shit for me. Big Mom, Mia and Aunt Rhonda took your place," he glared and his words cut her deeply.

"Boy, they can't never be your momma! I brought you in this world and I'll take you out!" she said pissed that the child she bore was being so disrespectful to her in her face. She approached him with authority in her eyes and raised her hand to slap him, but he warned her.

"If you put your hands on me, I swear to God, I'ma hurt you!" Tommy painfully assured her. And the look on his face spoke a million words -- he was dead serious.

It did however hurt him at first to say these things to his mother, the woman he loved, but he blanked that part out. To him, she was just like them, another crackhead, and he was going to treat her like one until she treated herself like something other than that.

Candice was crushed. And instead of it motivating her to want to change and get it together, his words only supported the way she felt already -- that she was a crack head, and that's all it was. So she spun on her heels and walked down to the strip with the other whores and flagged the potential "Johns".

Tommy shook his head in disgust. He tried hard to find even the slightest glimmer of what used to be his beautiful mom -- the one with the oval face and wide set almond eyes -- but that person was long gone. She now looked like a battered woman way beyond her years.

Tommy and Mike continued up the block after the confrontation with his mother. Mike wanted to say something to him about the way he was talking to his mother, but decided against it. He'd probably react the same way if his mom was on drugs, so he partially understood. He thought nothing else about it.

As they neared the house, they knew it was the one they were looking for. There was so much traffic running back and forth in and out the house, it looked as if someone was giving away free testers.

"Yo, I bet that's it," Tommy was amazed at all the traffic.

"Me too," replied Mike, and they headed up to the front door and knocked.

"Go 'round back!" the voice yelled from beyond the door, and they did as they were told.

They slid around the side of the house by way of the same alley in which the traffic flowed. They tried their best to make themselves look as if they were used to the whole scene, but their curiosity wouldn't allow them to as their eyes roamed. There were people lined up in the alleyway waiting their turn to get to the backdoor to buy their crack. It was amazing to them, not just at how they were waiting for the drug, but *who* was waiting for the drug. They saw Coach Cliff from the Boys' Club standing out here wide-eyed. They saw Ms. Thelma (cool ass B's mom), and some other people they never imagined to be standing in this alleyway. When they saw Tommy and Mike making their way through the alley, their first initial reaction was to put their heads down in shame. But after the eye contact, it was back to normal for them. They waited to get high.

When Tommy and Mike finally made it through the alleyway past the people waiting, Uncle Bear was waiting on them.

He snatched the door open the moment he saw them from the back window where he sat.

"Hey nephews! Whass'up? Y'all ready to do this?"

"Yeah, we ready," they answered together.

"Well, why y'all standing out there? Bring y'alls asses in," he said, and stepped aside so they could come in.

The house looked almost abandoned. The kitchen where they were at only had a table and four chairs around it, and it was almost spotless, probably because nothing had been cooked or eaten in here since the owner, Kelly, had started smoking. Smoking crack that is.

Kelly and her man stood over by the pantry in almost a huddled position as they smoked the crack cocaine. It was the first time Tommy and Mike ever seen someone in real life smoke coke, and to them it was kind of crazy to watch. They watched as Kelly held up to the end of her man's pipe what looked like a small blowtorch. He inhaled for a few seconds and blew out the smoke. That's when it got scary. His eyes got wide as 50 cent pieces, and his mouth twisted and moved rapidly, as his lips puckered up and got stuck that way. He grabbed a knife off the countertop, backed up against the wall and peeked out the curtains.

"Here they come! Don't let them in, Kelly! Here they come!"

"Man, sit'cha dumb ass down!" Bear snapped. "I don't know why dat nigga keep gettin' high if he can't control it!"

"That's what I be tellin' him, Bear," Kelly said. "I ain't givin' his dumb ass nothin' else!"

"Whass wrong with him, Unc?" Tommy asked.

56

"Yeah, why he lookin' on the floor and shit?" added Mike.

"'Cause dat nigga buggin!" Bear replied

Tommy and Mike jumped straight in, knee deep, and ready to get their hustle on.

Chapter Eight

One Man's Death, Two Men's Births

The next few months for Tommy and Mike were like drug dealer's boot camp. Uncle Bear had left them out to dry with the wolves. *What better way to learn than hands on experience,* he thought, and was pleased with his decision. By making that choice, he got a first hand preview of what his two nephews were made of and he liked what he saw.

They were real money-getters. They hugged the block like Newport butts; they were always there. There were times that Bear would have to make them leave the block, or they'd never leave the crackhouse. They loved making money. Bear's every nine day re-up had changed to every four days and money was rolling in like high tides from the ocean.

Things were going smoothly. However, along with the good, there was some bad, and losses came in bulk. Like the time when the connect sold Bear some bullshit. He sold him one brick of the regular good cocaine and a brick of some Bolivian shit to stretch it, and the smokers didn't like the taste. It took nearly two weeks alone to sell the garbage, and Bear was looking for another connect.

Then there were the little losses -- the ones Tommy and Mike took on the regular the first month of their induction. Being new to the game, they were subjected to all the slick shit they weren't used to, and the smokers were having open season on them. They were doing shit like asking them for four and five caps at a time, then changing their minds giving them the capsules back, only they switched the real ones with some fake ones in the same color capsules.

Then there were the times in a rush when they would say, *"Give me a twenty,"* (meaning four caps) and hand them some balled up money. They paid it no mind at the time because there were ten other motherfuckers with money and they wanted to get them out of the way because crowds drew suspicion, and the police. It would be later, after they shut shop down and started counting the money that they found out those few twenties they sold for the balled up money were actually $1 bills. They vowed to never let it happen again.

■■■■■■

It was a normal day at the job for Tommy and Mike. Like always, they hit the block promptly after school. They were enjoying their new life as hustlers because people started recognizing them, especially the girls in school. There was something different about them besides the noticeable change in their wardrobes. It was their maturity level. They had turned into little men.

When they walked inside Kelly's house, she was the only one there besides Bear. Tommy and Mike both had talked about Kelly on more than one occasion because they both secretly had a thing for the woman old enough to be their mother. Kelly was a bad motherfucker despite her crack addiction. She was different from all the other women they saw on crack, because like them, Kelly didn't lose weight and she kept herself up. They figured Kelly was in her first stages of addiction and hadn't entirely gone all out yet.

"Hey y'all," she spoke to them on entrance and flashed a smile at them. She knew they were infatuated over her. She could see it in their lustful, young eyes. So to tease them some more, she switched her phat ass out the kitchen and looked back at them right before she left out, only to catch them staring at her rear end. She smiled. *"I still got it!"*

■■■■■■

Bear left his nephews in the house with the last hundred bundles of caps. He figured that the bundles would last long enough for him to go to the mall, pick Mia up from work and go home to get some bundles to bring back.

He walked up Bennett Street towards 10th Street and waved at the brothers in Jesse & James Barber Shop on the corner, then turned up 10th Street and headed towards Sherman Street where he always parked his car. He ran his hand over his growing waves as he passed the place he'd been getting his hair cut for years and said to himself, *I need a cut.*

■■■■■■

"Hey, isn't that Bearacus Good?" the white officer asked as they rode up Bennett Street and were about to cross 10th Street.

"It looks like him," his Black partner sided with him.

"Well let's go see what he's up to then," the white officer said, and the Black officer backed the car up and directed it up 10th Street.

"Five-0 comin' up!" a lookout yelled from the corner of 10th and Kirkland Street, causing Bear to look back over his shoulder. When he saw the squad car coming up on his side, he paid it no mind. He wasn't dirty or anything like that -- he just had a lot of money on him -- but so what? If they decided to take it, he'd have his lawyer on it A.S.A.P. He continued turning onto Pine Street and walked half a block to Sherman Street and the cops were still on his side. They were going the same speed as he was walking and knew they were about to start fucking with him.

Damn, I hate these mu'fuckas! Bear said to himself when he saw who the officers were. It was Mitchell and Gamble, better known to the hood as "Dick and Head".

"Hey there, Mr. Good. What's going on? Or, how you say it... 'Whass up?'" the white officer asked sarcastically.

■■■■■■

Tommy walked outside to let the touters know that shop was open. A touter is a crackhead or junkie that is too lazy to go out and get their own hustle going, so they rely on other hustlers. They wouldn't boost, work or steal petty shit like hygiene products or anything. Instead they just hung around the block all day and brought dealers people looking for drugs. That was their job, and after they bought five different sells to the house they got paid in drugs for their work.

Tommy came back in the house and Kelly was sitting at the table talking to Mike. She caught Tommy's lustful eye as he came in.

"...Like I was saying to Mike, Tommy, I know y'all got the little young girls turned out in school, huh?" Kelly enticed them both. She had to admit it to herself too, because the two young bucks were sharp.

Tommy was dark-complexioned and had the whitest teeth and eyes you'd ever seen. *This probably the way Wesley Snipes used to look as a young boy,* Kelly thought, *Wit' his sexy ass!*

Mike, on the other hand, was caramel-complexioned, with his cute dimples, perfectly straight teeth and a head full of waves. He looked like a younger version of Usher.

"I'm tellin' you," Kelly continued, "If I was y'alls age again, I'd be all over y'alls asses. You hear me?" She paused after saying "hear", then threw the line out with the hook on it by saying "me". Then she got up and left the room.

"Damn! Yo, you see dat cousin?" Tommy whispered loud enough for Mike to hear.

"I know. Man, I'd wear dat ass out!"

"Me too!" Tommy replied. Truth was, they were both still virgins.

"Whass'up? You think we can get her to give us some?"

"I don't know. Why? You gon' ask her?" Tommy asked.

"Ask me *what*?" Kelly asked, catching them in the middle of the conversation. They both got silent. "Ask me what?" she repeated.

Fuck it, Mike thought before saying, "Whass'up?"

"*Whass'up?* What'chu mean, whass'up?" she asked, knowing already.

"You know," he said bashfully.

"Know what? Tommy, what he talkin' about?" she asked, involving him too, but he was as nervous as Mike was. He just shrugged his shoulders, gesturing that he didn't know what Mike was talking about, so she helped him out. "Look, how y'all ever gonna get what you want if y'all don't ask for it?" That was just the lead that they needed. Mike jumped at the opportunity.

"We wanted to know what was up wit'chu? You know what I mean? We wanted to know if you know... we could... um... get some... you know..." Mike tried to be straightforward.

"Some 'um what? Some pussy?"

"Yeah, some pussy." Mike repeated the word "pussy" and it came out easier now that she said it.

"What' chu gonna give me?"

"We got 'chu."

"I want a bundle from you, and a bundle from you, and y'all better not say nothing," she demanded.

"Dat's what's up!" they replied.

Kelly grabbed the bundles from both of them and safely tucked them away in the drawer by the sink.

"Make sure the doors are locked," she cautioned to Tommy before saying, "Come on." And they followed her upstairs. Kelly led them to the room all the way in the back of the house and stepped inside the doorway. "Come on," she said again without concern of her man catching them. Tommy and Mike did just that.

Inside the room the sun was shining brightly through a window with no curtain, just a fan in it. A small bed, no larger than a full-size, sat in the corner unmade. The sheets were clean, like Kelly was. It was the only part of her dignity that she wouldn't allow her addiction to take. She took pride in the way she looked because she figured if she could fool you with her looks, you wouldn't know just how fucked up she really was. And it worked. Looking at Kelly, you couldn't tell she smoked crack at all, unless you smoked with or in the same house she did.

"So whass'up? Which one of y'all want to go first?" she asked, stepping out of her clothes. They got rock hard. Tommy looked to Mike, and Mike looked to Tommy. Both were unsure of the answer. "Well?" she insisted.

"We both want to go," Mike answered.

"At the same time?" she asked.

"Yeah," he replied.

"Well come on then," she answered, stark naked only in her thong. "But first look in my pocketbook and get those condoms 'fore I end up pregnant by one of you fertile little cuties."

Tommy and Mike took off all of their clothes and walked over to the edge of the bed where Kelly now sat butt naked. She took the condoms from them and held them in her hands as she started on Mike first. Kelly leaned into Mike and gently placed his erection in her mouth as her free hand stroked Tommy's erection. She stopped on Mike and began on Tommy, sliding her lips around his tool and working her neck with no hands as she moaned and slurped as she gave head. "Mmmm!" she moaned. "Damn, you gotta big dick! Both of y'all!" She stroked their egos. "You sure y'all only fifteen?" she kidded.

"Mmm-hmm," Tommy moaned out an answer as his eyes rolled up in his head.

Kelly continued the head job on Tommy while she tore one of the rubbers from the pack and put it on Mike. All this head she was giving Tommy had the spot between her legs soaked, and she wanted some satisfaction too. "Come on," she said, pulling Mike by the dick as she positioned herself doggy-style on the bed. Mike climbed behind all that ass and palmed it like a basketball as his fingers sunk into that ass as if it were jelly in a bag. "Hmmp-mmm! Not there, baby, that's the wrong hole," she motioned and reached behind her to grab his dick. She glided it into her and instantly he felt the warmth of her body wrap around the condom as he stroked aimlessly.

"Damn, that feels good," he moaned and started to stroke faster. The clapping sound of his thighs smacking up against her ass only made the fucking session more intense.

All Tommy could think of was himself behind that ass, so he said, "Come on, cousin, let's switch."

And they did.

They balled Kelly's ass up in so many different positions that she forgot what to be fucked real good felt like, and she was loving it! The two young boys were definitely holding it down to be virgins, and she was cumming to the point she was drained.

Damn, these young boys got it goin' on! she thought as she moaned, screamed, pulled the sheets and grabbed at the air as she reached another orgasm. *Next time they gonna get this pussy for free!* That was a promise.
■■■■■■

Meanwhile, Bear was still having problems with the law…

"I'm doin' fine. Why?" Bear asked as he reached in his pocket for his car keys.

"I see," the Black officer said. "By the look of your rims and car, fine should be an understatement."

"You can get one too." Bear winked, unlocking the car's doors. "Are you done wit' me? I got other shit to do. And, don't y'all have better shit to do than fuck wit' me? You two mu'fuckas need to find a real job, or go get some pussy or sumptin'," he antagonized them and that agitated the officers.

"You fuckin' know what? You're a fuckin' smart ass!" the white officer, Gamble said, as Mitchell, his partner put the car in park.

A few people walking up the street stopped when they saw the officers getting out of the car. By the looks of things it was going to be a classical Black police officer showing out for the white cop by the way the Black cop charged around the car towards Bear.

"Put your hands on the car!" Mitchell, the Black cop said.

"For what?" Bear snapped, and Mitchell reached out and grabbed Bear's arms.

Bear snatched away. "Get da fuck offa me!"

"Get your hands on the car!" he said again, this time becoming more aggressive.

"Get your hands off of him!" one of the onlookers said.

"He ain't do nothin'!" another finished the sentence, and before you know it there was a crowd forming around the scene.

"Get back!" Gamble ordered the hostile crowd.

"Fuck you, white boy!" someone yelled, turning him beet red.

"I said get da fuck up off me!" Bear snapped, grabbing the cop around the shoulders. Officer Mitchell yanked away and threw a hard, but lazy punch that Bear ducked. When he came up he threw his own combination that dropped Mitchell to his knees. Mitchell was knocked out on his knees holding onto Bear's legs in an effort not to fall back.

Bear cocked back his hands and was about to finish him off when someone yelled, "BEAR! WATCH OUT!"

Bear heard the shout from the crowd, and attempted to do just that -- watch out.

Gamble was so petrified at the crowd's participation he became rattled under pressure. This wasn't some practice at the police academy, this was real. He panicked. "Get back!" he shouted out to the rowdy crowd.

"Fuck you, white boy!" was what came back, so he drew his firearm.

"Get back I said!" he yelled again, and this time he got some compliance. But that was interrupted by someone yelling, "That's right, Bear! Fuck his ass up!"

Gamble turned around only to see his partner dropped to his knees. He threw his pistol back in the holster, grabbed his blackjack and swung it with the intention to do some bodily harm. Unfortunately, the bodily harm proved fatal to Uncle Bear. He was caught in the back of the head with Gamble's blackjack.

The nightstick cracked his medulla (the brainstem connected to the spinalcord) and killed him instantly. Gamble called for paramedics and back up.

■■■■■■

Tommy and Mike were all smiles when Kelly came back with the soapy washcloths.

"Here," she said, handing them the warm rags with suds on them before adding, "Y'alls a mess!"

They didn't respond. They were too busy staring at her ass as it shook and bounced like a bowl of Jell-O.

"Damn, dat ass phat!" Tommy said with his face cringed up with approval.

"And dat pussy good too!" Mike added.

Truth was, he didn't even know if it was good or not, and neither did Tommy, because it was their first shot. They watched her ass jump up all the way down the hall until it disappeared into the bathroom. Instantly, Kelly had turned them out.

As they cleaned themselves up and got dressed to go downstairs to open up shop, they heard sirens off in a distance. They didn't pay it any mind until they heard, *"Boom! Boom! Boom!* the sound of someone banging the door in.

"Tommy! Tommy! The cops killed Bear, man! They killed your Uncle Bear!" he heard someone yelling from outback.

What? Tommy questioned himself. *That couldn't be right.* No, he hadn't just heard what they said. His Uncle Bear couldn't be dead.

"What?" Mike panicked. He lifted the back window up and hung his head from it and asked again, "What 'chu just say?"

"I said they just killed Bear! The mu'fuckin' police killed Bear. It was that mu'fuckin' dirty ass cop, Gamble," he said again before turning and running off. There was no mistaking what he said that time. They heard the words loud and clear.

Uncle Bear was dead.

■■■■■■

By the time they made it around to Sherman Street, it was jammed packed on the block. People were snapping! Nearly half the force had to be called out to keep the rowdy crowd from

68

rioting. But there wasn't enough of them to keep the crowd from yelling obscenities and throwing bottles. A few arrests had to be made before people starting getting the point and calming down.

Tommy and Mike couldn't see through the crowd, there were just too many people, so they pushed their way though. As they neared the chaos, Tommy heard screams. His heart thumped with fear. The screams were too familiar. It was Big Mom's screams. They sounded deafening, like her soul was being ripped away from her.

"*My baby!*" she screamed, "*Noooo! Not my baby! Lawd, why'd they kill my baaaaby?*" she screamed to heaven.

Mike started to tear up and Tommy did too at the pleas of Big Mom, but they didn't cry. They were soldiers. Bear had taught them to be stronger that that. They had to hold it down now. Hold down everything that Bear worked so hard to establish.

When they finally reached the actual scene, they caught the tail end of the paramedics pulling the white sheet up over Bear's face. He was gone.

One man's death equaled two men's births.

To

"NASTY"

Chapter Nine

The Nasty Years - 1997

Tell "G" I love my daughter... ♪
♫ If it was up to me,
She would be wit me, Sorta like ♫
Daddy Dearest...
♪ My visions be da clearest...
Silencers... so you can't hear it... ♫
Competition to the fearest
♫ Shit --
Don't ask me...
I went from ashy -- to nasty -- to classy! ♪

"Downfall"
Life After Death – "Biggie"

The pearl-white Lexus LS450 sedan sat pretty on the 20" Chrome B.B.S. rims. Tommy Good, the most notorious drug dealer in Wilmington's city, sat in its cockpit and cruised its huge body down 9th Street -- his street.

He and his boy, Mike had every corner from Clifford Brown Walk all the way down to Church Street, jumping with twenties of powder cocaine and chunks of hard white crack that had the smokers fiening for another blast of its potency. At twenty years old, five years after the death of Bear, he had doubled his stash fives times over. He was well on his way to becoming the youngest millionaire on the east coast in the game.

He owned two shops -- a beauty salon and a massage parlor. His cousin, Theresa ran the beauty salon, and Kenny managed the massage parlor, while Duck Butter, an ex-stripper broad that Tommy used to knock off, ran an illegal prostitution ring inside of the parlor. It was no secret how Duck Butter got her name either. Because everyone who had seen her -- and I do mean *everyone* -- for the first time said, "Damn! She phat like duck butter!" And the name stuck.

Tommy Good had become as cold as a December morning, and his icy cold temperament had the feel of the Arctic. It was very unpleasant and could be deadly if you crossed it. He had often asked himself, *Did Uncle Bear know he was going to die?* The answer to that remained to be the question. He remembered Uncle Bear telling him that if something happened to him, people would try to take what he started. He told them that they would have to rep (represent) Bennett Street to the fullest. It just so happened that they (he and Mike) were representing the whole east side of Wilmington, and some other parts.

Just as he was warned, now came the whispers that Bear was talking about. Already someone was planning or plotting to rob one of them, either him or Mike. He wasn't sure which one, but he had a surprise for whoever it was.

Now the tables were turned. Tommy had been warned. Now, instead of them getting robbed, they were going to rob the robbers. They weren't going to rob them for their money or any of their valuables though, because they had enough. They were going to rob them of their lives.

People thought that because Tommy and Mike were solo and had no team to back them, they thought they were vulnerable. Truth was they didn't want a team or a posse. *"No friends -- just family,"* was their motto. Why? Because friends let you down. It never failed. They would always disappoint you. That's why they had none. Strictly business, never personal. They figured who needed help when they were already sick. That's how they looked at life. Besides, no one was willing to go where they would if need be. They would go all out. There was no limit to what they'd do for one another or to protect what Bear had left behind.

You lived and you died, and that's all it was.

They had feelings for no one, except for family, and that's where he was going now, over to Ronett's. She was the one who called him with the news.

Tommy cruised down 9th Street, leaning back into the cool leather seats and listened to Biggie Smalls while the sun and humidity had the outside air feeling like an oven. He waved his hand at Ms. Rosemary, Big Mom's friend, sitting on her porch bathing in the hot July sun, and thought about his grandmother. Big Mom was getting older but she was still going strong.

It pained him to think about anything happening to her, but the reality was that one day we all must go, so he took it in stride. He had lost so much in his young life and been exposed to so much hardship that he was numb. Everything from his mother smoking crack, to not having a father around to losing a childhood friend (Michele), all the way down to losing Uncle Bear. So how could he be anything else other than numb? He couldn't. That's why he was so cold-blooded.

He'd rather Big Mom just go on and pass away now than to stick around and suffer. Then he wouldn't have to keep worrying about her, wondering how she was doing, wondering if she took her medicine, wondering when he would get that call. And, most importantly, who was going to pay for the funeral? Would his aunts and uncle pitch in when that time came, since Uncle Bear, the moneyman, was gone? He worried about all those things, and it was driving him crazy. He was tired of thinking about it.

Tommy turned his LS onto Church Street and headed over the 11th Street Bridge to the Buckett Projects where Ronett lived. In a couple of years though, to everyone's surprise, the Bucket would be torn down and made into townhouses. Its new name would be called "B2K, The Bucket 2000".

■■■■■■

"So what she gonna do? Put you out?" the boy named Oscar asked.

"Hell no, nigga! My love is king!" Shawn replied.

"So what happen? How'd she hear you?"

"I don't know. All I know is when I came out the bathroom she snapped! She said, *'Mutha'fucka ain't nobody goin' to do shit to my cousin! You must got da game fucked up!'* I said, *'Fuck your cousin!'* And she said, *'No! Fuck you, nigga!'* and that was it. I bounced."

"Then what?"

"Then she was standing at da door cryin', talkin' 'bout *'come back'*," he laughed.

"Do you think she gon' tell'em?"

"I don't know, and I don't give a fuck! Fuck Tommy and dat nigga, Mike. I want dat change, nigga! Is you wit' me or not?"

"Nigga, you know I am," he replied.

Shawn and Oscar were boys who grew up together on the north side of Wilmington. Twenty-seventh and West was their stomping grounds. Only they were different that most hustlers. They blew weed, got drunk, hung out, brought clothes, impressed the bitches and everything else that came along with the game, but they stayed frontin'. These niggas were running in place – stuck, hustling backwards and couldn't get right. Their only way to come-up was by sticking somebody up. So that was their game plan. It would have been useless to rob some street corner nigga, so why not go for the gusto? They knew several niggaz who were getting money too, but they decided to start with Tommy and Mike.

Shawn was Ronett's baby daddy, so he knew for sure that he could get Tommy to trust him. And even if she did tell him about what she had heard, Shawn would just deny it. *"Man, you know how it is?"* he pictured himself saying to Tommy. *"Baby mom's be trippin'. She just sayin' dat 'cause we beefin'. Why would I want to do sumptin' to you and you my girl's people?"* *Yeah, he'd go for that shit,* he told himself, and looked Oscar in the face, "Yo don't say shit to nobody! People run their mu'fuckin' mouths too much."

"I'm not," Oscar gave his word.

"You better not, 'cause if we… I mean, 'cause if they find out we did it, we gonna have to go to war with these niggaz, and that's too much unnecessary focus for nothin', feel me?"

"I feel you," he replied, and reached under the porch on the house on 27th and grabbed a potato chip bag. Inside was bag of weed. The car stopped right in front of them, and the girl behind the wheel asked, "Yo, who got weed?"

"Right here, baby girl," he said, and served her a bag before she pulled off.

"See what I mean?" Shawn asked Oscar.

"What?"

"Ain't nobody try'na be petty hustlin' and penny-pinching forever," he said, unsatisfied with his lifestyle. "A nigga try'na come up! And we will as soon as we knock Tommy and the rest of those niggaz off!" He had it all planned out. Everything, except when he would do it.

Chapter Ten

Now They Wanna Grab They Guns And Come Get You

Tommy sat in the living room and listened to Ronett ramble on about Shawn, her baby's daddy. Some of the shit she said was exaggerated, but most of the shit was on point. Shawn wasn't doing what he was supposed to be doing -- like taking care of the bills and shit. He wasn't spending time with her or their son. All he was doing was laying up, and she was getting tired of it.

Tommy made a note to make sure he confronted Shawn on the issues until they became dead issues to him. He had forgotten everything Ronett had just told him the moment she started talking about the conversation she overheard.

Ronett had been ear hustling on the telephone earlier when she heard Shawn and Oscar's plan to rob her cousin and Mike. They were going to call Tommy and ask to buy some weight off of him. "A half of a kilo," Ronett said, but Tommy knew they weren't built like that. He would be surprised if those niggaz had $10,000 between the both of them.

"...And that's what they said. Then I hung up. When he came downstairs I snapped!" she said, her voice becoming louder. "I said, *'You got the game fucked up! A mutha'fucka ain't gonna do shit to my cousin!'* He said fuck me and my cousin. Then he left."

"Where he at now?" Tommy asked.

"Probably up Market Street."

"On 27th?"

"Probably, but don't say nothin' to him about it, okay? Just tell the mutha'fucka he better start helping out with the bills and shit."

"I ain't gonna say nothin' to him. Dat nigga is a petty nigga! I don't know why you fuck wit' dat nigga anyway. All these niggaz out here be try'na holla at 'chu."

"'Cause I love'em, Tommy."

"Love'em my ass! Love don't pay no mu'fuckin' bills, I do." And he was right. Tommy and her were like brother and sister. He did everything since he was getting' it.

Maybe it was time for her to find someone else. Shawn was off balance all the time. Ronett was even starting to give up on herself. She had some shit she wanted to do for herself, like go to college, University of Delaware or Delaware Technical, to began a career in something, but that shit was on pause because she was always chasing behind Shawn's unmotivated ass. *Fuck dat, I want better for myself!* she thought when Tommy stood up to leave.

"You been to see Big Mom?" Tommy tried to keep the family tight.

"No, but I called her yesterday."

"Alright. Why don't you take your son over there to see her?"

"I will. Oh, and I seen Aunt Candice." Her eyes were planted on him to see his reaction.

"Where you see her?"

"Over there buying some drugs. I made her come over here and eat -- her and Lester. They looked bad."

"That's her dumbness. If they wanna keep getting high, let 'em. I'm tired of 'em."

"That's still your mom. You shouldn't treat here like that. Aunt Candy is my girl. She crazy as a mu'fucka. She keep me laughin'."

"Oh, wit'out a doubt. Yeah, that's my mom and I love her. She just needs to get her shit together."

"She will."

"I heard that before many times."

"Oh, before you go, lemme hold a few dollars so I can get my hair and nails done," Ronett begged.

Man, go to the shop and tell Theresa to hook you up. You don't need no money."

But I do need money. I have to buy my hair," she lied.

"Yeah, right!" Tommy uttered, but still passed off $200.

■■■■■■

"Damn nigga, what? I caught you at a bad time or sumptin'?"

"Oh, nah, you ain't catch me at a bad time. You know how me and my baby do. We stay role playin'," Mike laughed.

"What 'chall doin' now?"

"Runnin' around the house ass-naked, playin' hide-n-go-get-it. 'Member we used to play dat shit when we was kids?"

"Where y'alls kids?"

Mike had knocked up Ann twice. They had a son named Maurice and a daughter named Asia.

"They in daycare."

"Man, y'all is crazy as hell," Tommy laughed at them and quickly changed the subject before Mike started thinking about Michele as he normally did when he spoke of their childhood. "Yo, you know I just came over from Ronett's house and she told me that her sucker-ass baby daddy talkin' 'bout try'na rob us."

"What? Man, I'll murder dat nigga, and then take his son in like he mine. He too young to remember da nigga anyway. And I'd hate for the little nigga to have to grow up like *'dis is my dad?'* after learning his dad ain't shit!" he joked, but he was dead serious.

Mike's days of killing dogs, cats and anything else that had life in it was over. The game was real now. He was killing people, and he already had three under his belt.

"That's what I'm sayin'. These niggaz don't know who they fuckin' wit'."

"So whass'up? How many permanent resting places a nigga need?" Mike was ready to prepare a place for them.

"Just two...that's all... just two," Tommy repeated.

"Ai'ight then, come get a nigga tonight soon as it gets dark."

"Ai'ight." Tommy made it official and hung up.

■■■■■■

Tommy pulled up in an old Chevy Celebrity, the kind the undercover police used to drive. As soon as the moon appeared in the sky, he blew the horn and waited patiently for Mike to come out. He figured he and Ann was doing some kinky shit. They were perfect for each other, and Tommy was happy for his boy. They had been together since his 12th birthday.

Tommy smiled at the memory, because he remembered it clearly. He remembered his boy, Mike walking up to Ann and asking her to dance. Then he remembered them slow grinding to a slow song, with his country ass, while he slow danced with Davita. Tommy laughed at the thought. Then Davita flashed through his mind. *I wonder what she doin'? Do she still live in D.C.? I should ask Latoya about her? Nah, she probably don't even remember me.*

Tommy had been looking for a girl like Davita ever since she left, and no one he met could even come close to her. He had been with and fucked more than enough bitches to have at least have found one that compared to her, but he didn't.

Davita was his first love and no one ever could compare to that. *She probably got kids now and everything,* he thought. He pressed the CD's eject button, tired of listening to Tupac's *Makavelli*, and to his surprise it was "Old School Wednesday". The next song that came on was *Make It Last Forever*, by Keith Sweat and all he could remember was Davita singing the words in his ear:

"...Boy, I really need you/Baaaby, Baaaby, Baaaby/I'll make it all right..." he sang.

I need you too, he thought, and turned the radio up, leaned back and closed his eyes. Davita was there in his mind as he reminisced. If he ever met up with her again, he vowed to never let her go.

Damn, nigga! What you got, a bitch or sumptin'? All this love making music!" Mike banged on the window.

"Nah, man. I'm just reminiscing like Mary J., feel me?" he said and tried to sing the words, " ...*And ever, and ever, don't let our love ennnnd...*"

"Nigga, you is crazy!"

"Yo, I was thinking 'bout old girl."

"Who?"

"Davita, nigga! Dat's who," he stated like Mike should have known the answer.

"You still thinking about her? Y'all were kids."

"Man, you know you can't ever stop thinking about your first love."

"I know, cousin. You see I'm still wit' mines."

"You damn right! I'ma see mines one day, and when I do, if she ain't all fucked up, I'ma wife that."

"Yeah, ai'ight, but fuck dat shit right now. We can talk about that later. We on some other shit right now," Mike said, thinking Tommy was talking crazy.

Tommy drove the Celebrity like an old man on a Sunday morning after just having his car washed -- slow -- and leaned down low. He checked their surroundings in the car they nicknamed "The Hearse", then headed to the highway.

They went through the neighborhood called Village of Crofton until they came to a prohibited area. Old Smalley Dam Road had been closed down due to flooding and major complaints from the neighbors. It was the perfect place for them to discard the new set of bodies. Tommy deadened the lights and smoothly drove down the road until they came to the "No Outlet" sign, and Mike got out. He opened the makeshift gate, then closed it as Tommy drove through. Mike got back in the car and rode with Tommy deep into the wooded area until they got far enough down in there where they were out of eyesight.

"Skkkwwwshhh! Skkkwwwshhh! Skkkwwwshhh!" the shovels sounded as they broke the earth's soil and threw the dirt in the Celebrity's trunk.

■■■■■■

The next evening as the sky was turning dark pink from the sun's setting, Shawn was stepping out of the shower with a towel wrapped around his waist. He headed into the bedroom where an overworked Ronett still laid in total bliss.

He smiled -- smiled because his pride had been stroked by his strong fuck game. It bailed him out of everything he was doing, whether it was cheating, staying out all night, or planning to rob her cousin, Tommy. *She's on my side,* he thought.

"Baby," he called out to her.

"Huh?" she asked.

"Whass Tommy's number?"

"Why?"

"'Cause I need to talk to him about sumptin'."

"About what?"

"About some business. Why?"
"*Why?* 'Cause you was talking about robbing him, that's why, and no, I'm not giving you his number."

"Baby, you know I was only talking dat shit. You heard what I said. We was talking about a whole bunch of other people too. Why would I rob Tommy anyway? Especially when I know he's going to look out for me. Shit, we like family."

Shawn was right, Ronett thought. They were like family. Besides, Tommy said he wasn't worrying about Shawn. Shawn'susual shit, so what harm could it do if she gave him the number? None, exactly! That's why she gave him the number.

■■■■■

The next few days had passed by without a phone call and Tommy was beginning to think Shawn and Oscar had changed their minds. However, he also knew Ronett wasn't lying about what she overheard. *They must've changed up a little bit, re-thought their original plan, or just realized who they were fuckin' wit'.*

Then his phone rang. Tommy looked at the number that popped on the screen and hadn't seen it before. The number was new. *Maybe it's Shawn,* he said to himself and answered it on the third ring. "Who's this?"

"Can I speak to Tommy?"

"Who's this?"

"It's Shawn."

"Shawn who?" Tommy played him.

"Ronett's Shawn," he answered.

"Oh, whass'up, cousin?"

"Ain't shit. Where are you?"

"All that ain't important, baby boy. You da police or sumptin'? Those the kind of questions the police ask, cousin. My phone may be tapped or some shit, yours too. Anyway, whass good?"

"You right! I'm try'na see you 'bout sumptin'."

"Enough said. This is your number right?"

"Yeah, dis my number."

"Ai'ight den, I'ma hit you as soon as I get in town. If you woulda called me earlier today I was right in town. I could've taken care of that."

"It's all good. I wasn't ready for you then no how, feel me?"

"Ai'ight, I'll holla. I'ma hit you when I get in town," Tommy affirmed and hung up the phone.

After the call, Tommy turned to Mike who was staring at him the whole time he talked on the phone, and gave him the nod.

"Let's do this!" Tommy was eager to get at Shawn's snake ass.

Instantly, Mike's adrenaline began to flow and his heart pumped faster. With each beat, a stream of cold blood pierced his veins, turning him into an alter ego.

Tommy turned onto I-95 and headed into the city. Inside the car two shovels and a container of deadly acid awaited Shawn and Oscar.

■■■■■■

When Tommy pulled up to their destination, he surveyed the area. There were just too many people outside to execute their plan, so he drove past the crowd. Mike wanted to just jump out and kidnap the niggaz, but with all the people outside Tommy decided they were sure to be cased up immediately if they made a move. It was 1997 and snitching was becoming the new wave of the future.

"Yo, why you ain't stop? There go them niggaz right there," Mike impatiently asked.

"Man, its way too many people outside."

"Man, fuck them people! Go back 'round da block. Nigga, we gonna set an example out these mu'fuckas! I bet don't nare 'nother mutha'fucka think 'bout disrespectin' us no more! I'ma expose the bitches in these niggas. Now pull this mutha'fuckin' car over!" Mike demanded as Tommy rounded the block.

Irrationally thinking, Mike jumped out the car with lightning speed. In his hands he gripped two chrome .44 magnums. The move he made was so sudden it caught everybody on the block by surprise.

"Look mutha'fuckas!" he began as he waved the guns aimlessly into the crowd of people who were scrambling for safety at the sight of them. "I want every last one of you mu'fuckas to pay attention, 'cause I'm dead mutha'fuckin' serious!" He spoke to no one in particular, but still continued to yell at the few that were left frozen in their tracks. "I want y'all to watch this shit. Pay close attention to this shit 'cause it could happen to anyone out this mu'fucka!

Shawn and Oscar halted because they assumed everything was cool. All they knew was Tommy's boy, Mike was going off. However, when Mike singled them out, they knew something wasn't right.

"You two bitch-ass niggas, come da fuck *here!* Y'all know who I'm talkin' 'bout, so don't make me come get you!" Mike demanded, but neither moved. When his demands were ignored, Mike lifted the .44 magnum and aimed it at Oscar's leg.

"BOOM!" The gun sounded and Oscar screamed like a bitch getting her virginity taken by a foot-long dick.

"Shut yo' bitch-ass up, nigga!" Mike snapped.

Sprinkles of onlookers were caught in the mix of dodging bullets.

Nigga, you came up wit' the bright idea to rob me and Tommy?"

Tommy had the trunk popped open, knowing that Mike was about to let the heat blast again. He watched as Shawn tried to plead his case.

"Nah, it's not like that, fam. I would never cross y'all! Tommy, you know me! We family! Call Ronett, she'll tell you I wasn't schemin' on you!"

At this time, Tommy pulled his pistol out and forcefully demanded that a wounded Oscar get in the trunk, and Shawn get in the back seat of the car. "Get yo' bitch-ass in the back seat, nigga! 'Cause this shit ain't gone be pretty, and that's my word." Mike was infuriated listening as this nigga, Shawn tried to talk his way out of death.

"That's my word! I put that on everything. Call Ronett!" Shawn contemplated on running, but changed his mind. He was too scared to run. He could already imagine the feeling of the bullet burning through his back if he ran off. Plus, he knew his chances of outrunning a bullet were slim to none.

"Come on, nigga! Let's go! Fuck what you talking' 'bout. Get in!" Mike shoved him after closing the trunk on Oscar.

"You's a mu'fuckin' gangsta, right? You in the mu'fuckin' game, right? You gon' take this shit like a man!" Tommy grilled him.

"Bitch-ass nigga!" Mike blurted, and smacked Shawn in the head with his pistol as Tommy peeled away from the scene.

Minutes after they pulled off, the Wilmington police arrived on the scene. Strangely, but not coincidently, no one uttered a word.

Chapter Eleven

Around The World, Niggaz Pay Me Dues...

It was over a month aftrer Tommy and Mike made an example of Shawn and Oscar. The whispers started spreading. There were all types of rumors circulating around the city about what happened to them. The funny thing about it though was that they were being kept to a minimum. Out of a small amount of respect but a great deal of fear, no one dared to leak informatin to the authorities. Tommy and Mike had the 'hood walking on eggshells and even other boss niggaz from other 'hoods were starting to hear rumors of the young duo. Their names were ringing bells in the underground from Delaware to Philadelphia, New Jersey to New York, and from Florida to California. Even a portion of their out-of-state connects heard bits of information.

Tommy and Mike were very much aware of the small talk from 'hood to 'hood. They always knew that a lot of shit came with being on top, but they vowed to stay there. This added another notch of street credibillity on their belts. This let mu'fuckas know they were willing to get their hands dirty if need be.

To stroke their egos even more, they copped new cars. Tommy bought the new smoked gray tinted silver Q-45 Infinity and rimmed it up. Mike, on the other hand, kept it sport. He bought the new BMW 850 CSi. The jet-black sports car almost looked like a shark on the streets, with its nose and rounded back.

And now people were really talking. They had the hottest wheels on the street. But that was only the beginning. They were climbing the ladder to success "escalator style". They managed to gorilla their way up to the top and no one even dared to challenge them. There was nothing else for them to do but count money and fuck bitches. Oh, and of course... count more money!

Chapter Twelve

So Far Away... But So Close In Heart

Johns Hopkins University of Maryland, located on Charles Street in the northern part of Baltimore city, was a historically known college and a standout for its School of Medicine. The University had turned out some of the most successful doctors in history, and Davita was determined to be one of next great podiatrists. The college life brought on new associates, but she still maintained a close relationship with her childhood friends back home in D.C.

Although her childhood friends thrived for success, Davita's goals were far more advanced than theirs. They were content with what they had. Not saying any of it was bad, but who wanted to be standing on their feet all day doing hair? It just wasn't the ideal job for her. Neither was running a daycare for children. She wanted more than that. She wanted to be able to shop at Gucci, Saks Fifth Avenue, Prada, Salvatore Ferragamo's, and all the other top designers, and not effect her budget. That's why she chose the medical field after high school. And now in her fourth year, she was more than half-way through. She could see her doctor's office door now, as the white letters trimmed in gold read "Dr. Davita Anderson". The thought made her smile and also more determined to succeed.

■■■■■■

Davita left her last class of the day drained as usual. This was one of the only nights she would really get a good night's sleep because she didn't have any classes to take tomorrow morning. She stopped down to the school's mess hall and ordered a cup of Bella Crema Gourmet Cappuccino, heavy on the sugar. She rarely drank dark liquid because they stained her teeth, but she was tired tonight. Her pearly whites would just have to forgive her this time because she sure wasn't about to fall asleep behind the wheel of her car. Her apartment was all the way across town. almost a forty minute drive.

At twenty-two years old, Davita was a bombshell. Even now, as she walked out the mess hall dressed in doctor's scrubs and a long white overcoat with her badge on the outer pocket, she was still stunning. Davita had sprouted up nearly 3, leaving her standing at a cool 5'9". Her slender but long build gave her the look of a model, and so did her facial features. Her neck was slim, long and very delicate looking, and her shoulders draped just right. Her face was oval and very much chiseled to perfection. She almost looked like a young Beverly Johnson. The years had been good to her. Davita was a grown woman. There were only three words that could describe her: *Damn, she fine!* And they described her perfectly.

Davita pulled up to her upscale apartment because it defined who she was. The complex was elegant -- she was elegant. There was a guard's tower at the entrance. There was huge fountain that sprayed water into a man-made pond, with tennis courts, basketball courts, a swimming pool and a fitness center that held aerobics classes and yoga. The place was beautiful, a picture taken right out of a *Better Living* magazine. It was more than enough for now, and she thanked her brother, Sinqué for being so generous to her all the time. It was because of him that she stayed in a $1,400 a month complex. But only until she finished school and began her practice. She would put her doctor's office right in the 'hood to help her people. And it would be good to give other young kids hope, especially knowing that she was once underprivileged like them.

Davita turned the key to the lock on her door and went inside. The comfortable two-bedroom apartment welcomed her as if it had arms, and suddenly she wasn't tired anymore. *It must be the coffee,* she reasoned and began vacuuming the floor. After that she did some light housekeeping and prepared for a long hot bath.

She contemplated touching herself, but then she'd be all worked up with no one the help her finish what she started.

Damn, how she missed Tyrone, her former love who broke up with her, and Davita was in agreement with the break up. It hurt them both to do it because they really enjoyed each other's company. The problem was they were headed in two different directions. She was in school trying to establish her very own career, while he was trying to make the cut to play national football. He had told her he was going to play for the Frankfurt Galaxy, an NFL European team. So that meant the end of their relationship. He was leaving for Europe and she wasn't willing to sacrifice for him.

"If it's true love," she remembered him saying, *"It'll come back."* What a liar he was.

When she finished bathing and putting on her pajamas to get ready for bed, she walked out to the living room and grabbed her photo album. She flipped through its pages and looked at pictures of her and Tyrone, remembering when every photo was taken. It felt good to reminisce. As she continued to flip pages, there were two pages of pictures from the summer of '89 when she spent it in Delaware with her cousin, Latoya, Aunt Cookie and Aunt Sandy. She remembered that summer because it was the first time she fell in love. His name was Tommy Good.

I wonder what he's doing... How's he doing? What about Mike? How'd he turn out after losing his twin sister the way he did?

She laughed aloud at the picture of tommy in the swimming pool. "Eeeewww! Look at those scrawny legs, just as ashy, and that chest. He knows he needs a shirt on. Look at that bird!" she continued to laugh.

Then her mood swung from happiness to depression as she thought about how long it had been since she had a kiss, been touched or loved by a man, or even in the presence of one for that matter. She wanted one now, but who? There was nobody. Tyrone was in Europe, and God only knew where Tommy was. So she had to do like always. Tonight she'd cuddle up with the blankets and listen to the radio.

She jumped in her bed, put on her favorite oldies but goodies station, and couldn't believe her ears. *Damn! Déjà vu!* she thought as Keith Sweat's *Make It Last Forever* sang her to sleep.

That night Tommy was in her dreams.

Chapter Thirteen

The After Party

The M.C.I. Center in the nation's capital was where it all took place. It was the last show of the year, the one between Christmas and New Year's, and it was all that it was cracked up to be. The year of 1997 had been a year to remember for Tommy and Mike and the hip hop world.

For them it marked the year they staked their claim. The year they reached $999,996 + $4 mo' dough -- a cool million-dollars -- a millionaire mark, and they were loving it.

For the hip hop world, it was a year that marked the death of hip hop's greatest rapper, the "Notorious" B.I.G., putting an end to the worst rap music beef of all time. The two greatest rappers, B.I.G. and Tupac Shakur, would be dearly missed for many years to come. Good thing there was a guy named Jay-Z on the wing. He was the most up and coming rapper in the game. And even when the two legends were alive, Jay-Z was making his mark. In many people's opinion, Jay-Z was the best rapper even then. Later on, longevity and continuous mic skills would prove these people right.

The show itself was a smash. The all-star cast that performed clearly made it the best show of the year so far. Jay-Z, Master P, The L.O.X., Snoop Dogg, and Lil' Kim turned it out. But the jump-off was the after party at club Dreams in D.C. DMX was the headliner.

Tommy drove the Hummer in circles around the nation's capitol in search of the nightclub. His stubbornness wouldn't allow him to pull over and ask for directions, but Mike was tired of the same shit.

"Yo, if you don't pull this mutha'fucka over and ask a mutha'fucka for some directions nigga, I'ma snap!" he joked. "We lost than a mu'fucka!" Mike finished.

Tommy just gave him a crazy look, but didn't respond. He was pissed off but he sure wasn't going to let Mike know. He hated admitting he was wrong, but he pulled into a gas station any way for assistance. Tommy walked inside and asked the cashier/gas attendant for directions. When he got back to his vehicle Mike was waiting to joke on his partner.

"Nigga, I wasn't even gonna say nothin' to you, but since you insist you were going in the right direction, I didn't say nothing. I knew you was lost twenty minutes ago."

"Man, fuck you nigga!" Tommy laughed back at him, getting back in the Hummer, this time getting them to Dreams within minutes.

When they pulled into the nightclub the line was long. Cars of every kind lined the sidewalks of the club, and the Hummer fit right in with the tops. But what set it off from the rest of the competition was that it was an all terrain vehicle and built for whatever Mother Nature threw at it. Tonight it was snow, so Tommy was glad he chose to drive it. The weather outside tonight was well below freezing and the crowd that came out was dressed to impress.

The nation's capitol, Washington, D.C., was the "Chocolate City" -- a district known for poppin' style and flashing fashions, and tonight it showed. The club poppers were sharp! They weren't going to let the little bit of snow stop them. Besides, it wasn't sticking anyway. The little that did stick wasn't much, but it did manage to paint D.C. into a perfect picture for a postcard, especially, for the holiday.

Tailor-made suits, matching furs, gator boots, two-piece suits like the boy Steve Harvey, and almost any other style you could think of. The niggaz had that shit on. The women were almost flawless, like a 5 carat VH diamond ring. Their body-fitting dresses, high heel stiletto boots and D.C. hairstyles had each one of them only one director away from Hollywood and a photographer away from being the next Tyra Banks.

Tommy stepped out of the Hummer in quarter-cut reptile boots made by Mauri, and a purple labeled suit by Salvatore Ferragamo. His silk tie was from the finest and tied loosely around his neck, while his animal hung on his body (his animal being his full-length mink, the color of midnight blue). His wrist was covered with a Presidential Rolex with a band so icy it looked like it could only belong to one mu'fucka -- Slick Rick.

Mike, on the other hand, kept it basic. Not too plain, not too flashy. He wore black slacks and matching sweater by Versace, and boots by Ferragamo. His watch was a twin to Tommy's, but his two pinky fingers were ridiculous. Mike had 10 carat pinky rings that glittered like a 1970's disco ball that hung over the center of a dance floor.

Mike reached for the small of his back and patted his two chrome .44 magnums, then tapped his chest. His vest was strapped on tightly, and so was Tommy's. Then they walked up to the club.

■■■■■■

"Girl, my hair ain't done!" Davita said, trying anything she could to get out of going to Dreams with her old neighborhood friends, Shaylynn and Yolanda.

"Bitch, you know damn well I'ma do your hair," Shaylynn argued.

"I don't know, girl. I ain't been out in so long."

"I know, bitch. Dat's why we want you to come out. You so caught up in them books and shit and cooped up in that damn house that you forgot how to live."

"It's an apartment."

"See what I mean? Bitch, you know damn well I know it's an apartment. You have really changed. Bitch, you remind me of some white girl or somethin'... you even talkin' like one. That school got you fucked up."

"I do not, and it does not."

"Da fuck it don't! Now find somethin' to wear, girl, 'cause I'm on my way. I'ma be gettin' dressed over there, and I'm bringin' my supplies. So wash your hair," Shaylynn ordered and hung up.

That was over three hours ago and one curl away from having her hair done up in a style that Shaylynn whipped up from scratch. She was the best in D.C. and Davita saw why she was doing well for herself. In fact, she was doing numbers. Shaylynn was averaging about $48 thousand a year -- very good for a hair stylist -- not to mention the rent she pulls in weekly from the six chairs in her shop, Shay's Cuttin' Up.

"There, bitch. Go look at dat," she boasted.

"Does everything that comes out of your mouth, Shaylynn, have to be derogatory?"

"Girl, I'm from the 'hood, unlike you. I'm in da shop all day long around this type of language."

"Does that mean you have to adopt it? I'm from the 'hood too."

"Correction: *Was* from the 'hood."

"Still am. I just choose to talk with some sense.

"No bitch, you choose to talk white. I'm not ashamed of how I talk. This is who I am. And bitch, I'll talk to your classmates like this, your professors, the dean and all those other siddity college mutha'fuckas you be wit'! I ain't changing for you or no one else. I pay my own bills, don't owe nobody shit and ain't gotta kiss ass to do it!" Shaylynn admitted, and Davita started questioning herself. Was she really changing?

"Now get me a towel and washcloth please." Shaylynn couldn't help but to laugh. Her words had scared the shit out of Davita. "Baby, I'm sorry. You ain't really change. You da same ole Davita. I just ain't been around you so long, girl. I miss you, dat's all. You are gettin' a little boushie though," she joked, and Davita tossed her the towel and washcloth.

"Thanks, girl, 'cause for a minute you had me questioning myself about some shit."

"Girl, you ai'ight!"

After Davita got dressed, she stood in front of her bedroom mirror and thought, *Damn! I forgot how getting dressed up made you feel!* Being dressed up could put you in a good mood, a real good mood. And that's what it had done for Davita. She looked absolutely remarkable in her body-fitting Cougi dress and red matching rider boots made of crocodile. Her hairstyle though, was what set it off. Shaylynn had tapered one side of her head and put a bang on the other side that covered her eye seductively, while the back still hung shoulder length. The cut was *bad* and it was original. She reached in her closet, grabbed her red mink and matching hat. They were ready to take on Chocolate City.

"You ready? Where's Yolanda?" Davita asked.

"Da bitch 'possed 'ta meet us dere," Shaylynn answered on purpose. "Yeah bitch! I said it!" she joked.

"Bitch, fuck you!" Davita said.

"Dat's the Vita I know!" Shaylynn said and gave her a high five as they left the house.

■■■■■■

The two of them were so close to one another but yet so far away from each other. She was in the V.I.P. with her brother, Sinqué (a.k.a. Hollywood as he was known throughout D.C.), while Tommy and Mike lingered in the crowd.

The V.I.P. section of the club was lavish. It had a food and fruit table set up as a number of seductive hosts walked around taking orders for people's drinks.

Davita was glad she had come out because she hadn't mingled with her peoples in a while, and the feeling was good. Just being in the presence of the stars made her feel important, especially when one of the rappers tried to get her number.

"Girl, is you crazy?" Yolanda tried to say, but was cut off by her girl, Davita.

"I know who it is."

"Girrrrl, he's sweatin' the shit outta you!" Shaylynn admired.

"I don't care, I'm not one of his groupie broads."

"Davita stop being so damn stuck up. You ain't never gonna find another Tommy Good," Shaylynn said, knowing her girl Davita been trying to find some Tommy Good in every man she met.

"Whatever," she responded and went back to mingling.

Sinqué was glad to see his little sister out enjoying herself, but he was upset. He had become among the most deadly drug dealers on the entire east coast, and as a result, D.C. and Baltimore had become the murder capitols. Hollywood ran the Murphy Homes Projects in Baltimore and the northeast part of D.C. with pure china white he sold on its street corners. Heroin ruled, and he ruled it. If a bag of dope was sold from D.C. to Philly, Hollywood got a piece of the money. That's why he was upset with his sister. He was a target, and now she was too. Niggaz would love to kidnap her from the streets and use her for ransom. That's why he kept her away in school out in the suburbs. No one would think to look way out there, but here she was, a sitting duck.

■■■■■■

Down on the dance floor and near the bar, Tommy and Mike were in the muck of the club. The few people who saw them come into the club had managed to start the whispers up about the two, especially since they saw the Delaware tags on their Hummer.

"Yo, Joe, I think that's the boy, Tommy Good and his boy, Mike," one hustler at the bar said when the two walked past.

"I know. You look at dat nigga's watch," the other hustler said to his boy.

"Girl, who is Tommy Good?" one girl asked her friend when she overheard the young hustlers talking.

"I don't know. It might be him right there," she said. "If it's him, dat nigga sharp!"

Tommy and Mike heard the whispers and felt the eyes on them as they made their way over to the bar. It was nothing that they weren't used to. They'd been getting looks from everyone everywhere they went now. They were ghetto superstars. It was just part of the territory.

As usual, Tommy and Mike avoided the V.I.P. section of the club like they did every club they went to. They did that because niggaz in V.I.P. were out of touch. They had let the money go to their heads and lost their edge, the side of them that got them to where they were. Tommy and Mike weren't going to let that happen, that's why they stayed mingling amongst the regular patrons -- the niggaz who were in the streets -- the ones who were on the corner. The ones barely flipping 4½ ounces a week -- the ones that were grimy. That's who they felt more comfortable around because it kept them on point -- kept them hungry. Moving kilos a week wasn't enough for Tommy and Mike; they wanted to move mountains.

They ordered a couple of drinks and turned to the stage and watched as DMX blazed *Where My Dawgs At?* The crowd went crazy.

Tommy looked at Mike when the chorus began and said, "Where my dawg at?"

Mike in return answered, "I'm right here, dawg." And they both smiled.

The song was their theme song for each other and the inspiration of their tattoos. On Tommy's left shoulder were the words "Where My Dawg At?" And on Mike's right shoulder was the words "I'm Right Here, Dawg!" And they meant it. They would be by each other's side until the death of them.

After DMX performed a couple of more songs, the party went back to normal. There was plenty of time to pull some ass.

Tommy insisted on keeping the party live. He called the bartender over to where he was and asked, "How much to buy the bar out? I want all the drinks to be free, you heard me?" he asked, but the bartender couldn't answer the question.

"I'll have to call the owner," he replied and picked up the black phone behind the bar. In minutes he was talking to his boss. "Uh, sir, there's a guy here inquiring about buying the bar out, and making it free drinks for everybody. Is that possible?"

"You damn right it's possible! You figure we'll pull in about two or three extra grand a night. Tonight it's a full house, so we might do double. So yeah, if he wants to buy the bar out, tell him to drop five thousand on the table. If he does, have Lisa bring the money to my office immediately!" he said and hung up.

"So what he say?" Tommy asked.

"Five thousand."

"That's all?" he sarcastically responded, and tossed one knot to him. "Have dat shit announced... free drinks for everybody! Compliments of the boy, Tommy Good!" he said and flashed a smile as he and Mike now sat at the head of the bar.

The next thing you knew the D.J. was on the microphone making the announcement:

"Party people in the house! Special shout outs to the nigga, Tommy Good, right there at the head of the bar!" he pointed. "It's because of him y'all that the drinks are now free! That's F-R-E-E! He bought the bar *out*!" the D.J. finished and turned the volume back up.

After that, everyone in the club knew who he was. Even the stars would remember that name, Tommy Good, the "Ghetto Superstar".

He looked up at the V.I.P. and around the club, and every pimp, playa, hustler, boss, star and bitch in the nightclub gave him a head nod or tipped a hat to the man of the night.

Chapter Fourteen

If It's True Love, It Really Does Come Back!

"**O**n my God, girl! Did he just say Tommy Good!" Davita asked amazed.

"Bitch, I don't know what they said his name was, all I know is that they said "free drinks" bitch, and I'm going to get mine!" Shaylynn eagerly stated to Davita just as excited as her girl. "I hope they did, 'cause I can't wait to see this Tommy Good character."

"Who they say?" Hollywood asked his sister.

"I think they said Tommy Good," she answered quickly.

The name rang a bell to him. "Tommy Good... Tommy Good?"

"Yeah."

"How you know this Tommy dude?" he curiously inquired.

"Remember that summer when I stayed in Delaware with Aunt Cookie and Aunt Sandy?" she answered, and the name registered instantly.

Tommy Good was the young boy that he kept hearing about, the one that was making all the noise up north around Delaware, Philly and New Jersey. It was said that he and his boy, Mike were the youngest millionaires in the game, at the ages of twenty.

"Oh, that's the boy Mommy said you was crying over. She said that you didn't want to leave and that you cried all the way to D.C. from Delaware," he teased his little sister.

"I did not!" She lied and he knew it. The spark she had in her eyes right now proved that. She was in love with whoever this Tommy was and her brother wanted to meet him. Not only to see why his sister was so flabbergasted about him, but because he was already thinking business.

"Well if that's him, bring him up here because I want to meet him," he said, and Davita crossed her fingers. She sure hoped it was him. Besides, how many Tommy Good's could there possibly be?

"Alright, damn! First you gotta go let me see." she said, tired of the small talk. "Come on y'all," she called to her girls, and pushed her brother to the side.

"Damn! Knock me over the next time," Hollywood joked, and grabbed a handful of Yolanda's ass as she walked pass.

"Yeah, it's still soft and phat to def *and is!* And the pussy still tight. Can take da rubber right off your dick, nigga!" she toyed with Hollywood, then kept it moving. She wasn't lying either and Hollywood knew it. The pussy was blazin' and he was going to get some more of it tonight.

Davita, Yolanda and Shaylynn left the V.I.P. room and headed downstairs to where the party was jumping.

"Damn! We shoulda been down here from the jump!" Yolanda said when they reached the dance floor.

"I know, huh? All these fine ass brothers down here," Shaylynn added, but Davita didn't respond with a comment of her own. Her mind was elsewhere. The only thing on her mind was praying that the name she heard them call was Tommy Good's, and that it was really him. *If it's not,* she imagined, as she made her way to the bar, *I'ma be heartbroken.*

For years Davita wondered about her first love, yearned for him at times, even masturbated to the many thoughts of them rubbing clothes together that summer, wondering if it would really feel that good. The way it felt as they kissed and grinded each other even now after having real sex, the feeling couldn't compare to the way they rubbed their clothes as children. Maybe it was a mental thing, but for the most part it did feel better. The closer she got up on the bar, the more she moved her neck, stood on her tiptoes and maneuvered her head trying to get a good look at the bar. And then she saw him -- saw a glimpse of his face at the bar when an opening opened up for a split second.

Oh, my God! It's him! she thought. Now she didn't know what to do. She stood stock still.

"Bitch, whass wrong wit' chu?" Why you just stop like dat?" Yolanda asked as she bumped into the back of her.

"'Cause girl, it's him!"

"Where he at?" Shaylynn and Yolanda asked in unison.

"Right there," Davita answered, and they looked at the legendary Tommy Good, the one that had their girl fucked up since they were kids. And they understood too. They still remembered their own first loves, but it was different for them. See, they grew up with their first loves and had the opportunity to get closer to them. They had an opportunity to grow up and grow apart from them, but they still remembered.

"Well, I know you gonna say somethin'," Shaylynn stated very loudly.

"I know you are too. As much as you talked about this nigga, Tommy Good! I know you betta go say somethin'. *Shiiit!* I could'a stayed up there wit' ya' brotha," Yolanda admitted, as much as she wanted to hit Hollywood off with some ass tonight.

"What am I supposed to say? What if he don't remember me? Girl, we were only twelve years old. He probably got a woman by now."

"Bitch, that's your real first love. Probably the only real love you'll have in your life again. You know why? Because it's based solely on love. It was genuine. It wasn't no money involved, wasn't a whole lot of material shit to get in the way. It was just the two of you. Everything was real and honest. Today, it's not like that. So bitch, I know you best go get yo' man, 'fore I do 'cause he's a big, pretty Black mutha'fucka! Look at those muscles! They fillin' out the shirt," Shaylynn said, giving her girl some words of encouragement.

"Y'all comin' wit' me?"

"Girl, you know we are. We wouldn't want to miss this reunion for the world!" Yolanda said.

"And I wouldn't want to miss that sharp ass nigga wit' him," Shaylynn said, and Davita smiled brightly.

She hadn't even paid any attention to who Tommy was with. It was her boy, Mike, and *Damn! Look how he's grown up! He don't look all country and slow now,* she thought, then said, "Girls, that's his boy, Mike!"

"Who's Mike?"

"Dat's my nigga! Come on y'all. Let's go," Davita advised, then added, "Before one of them bitches gets too friendly wit' my baby and I have to turn dis mutha…"

"Girl, watch 'cha mouth," Shaylynn and Yolanda said on cue.

"*Out!*" Davita finished, and they enjoyed a laugh.

"I would be jealous too. He fine as hell!" Yolanda agreed.

"I know that's right!" Shaylynn seconded as they headed over to Tommy and Mike.

■■■■■■

Tommy and Mike were at the bar feeling themselves, as they were surrounded by lovely ladies. Even the celebrities tonight in attendance paid them homage. They were the young bosses. And even DMXgave his nod to them. Tommy loved that part; DMX was his favorite rapper. And if he wasn't mistaken, he could have sworn Lil' Kim and the entourage of females with her was giving him the eye.

They were enjoying themselves to the fullest, as they tilted back bottles of champagne to Biggie's *Mo' Money Mo' Problems* song. Tommy bobbed his head to the music as it banged loudly out of the speakers, and on cue, right with the lyrics of the song, he and Mike lifted their bottles in the air. When they did, their sleeves fell back on their arms and revealed their Rolex's as Biggie sang, "*...Throw you Rollies in da sky/and wave 'em side to side...*", and that's just what they did.

Mike was in a groove himself, but he didn't let it stop him from being on point as always. He needed to stay focused on his surroundings because he knew where he was. He was in D.C., the "Chocolate City", the "Murder Capitol", home of the legend, "Hollywood".

Hollywood and his people were known killers. Their trademark was a Colombian necktie -- not a tie you wore, but the tie murder victims wore. The Colombian tie was when Hollywood would cut the throat of his victim -- mainly snitches and people who owed him money. Then after their throat was cut, they'd pull their tongue down through the cut and stretch from the neck, therefore making it look like a tie. That's how the name came about. The look was grotesque and stomach turning to even the hardest criminals. That's why Mike was on point. He didn't know if Hollywood was in attendance or not. And if he was, he sure hoped that he didn't take Tommy's buying out the bar as an act of disrespect. But if he did, Mike would be ready. He always was. Mike continued to let his eyes roam around the room, and then, out of nowhere she appeared out the clear blue. It was Davita.

"Oh shit, cousin! You ain't gonna believe this shit!" Mike said excited.

"Believe what, nigga?" Tommy said drunk, but not pissy drunk.

"There's Davita!"

"*Who?*" he asked, making sure he wasn't hearing things.

"Davita, nigga!" Mike said, and Tommy sobered right up.

"Where?"

"Right there."

Tommy looked in the direction Mike was looking in and saw her for himself. She was even more beautiful than he remembered her being. And she was coming his way. It felt as if the whole club had disappeared from around him and it was just him and her. The form-fitting Cougi dress hugged her body like a candy wrapper, revealing her impeccably shaped hips. The way she walked made them bounce and sway provocatively, as if she was walking in slow motion. Her red mink hung from her shoulder, revealing the shoestring straps on her dress and her beautiful neckline. The look was astonishing.

Tommy stared at her almost in a daze. And when their eyes met for the first time since that day he chased behind the car, he stood from his barstool and waited for her to greet him.

Davita jumped right into his open arms when he ran up to her. She wrapped her arms around his neck as he swept her off her feet. She lifted her feet off the ground and crossed her legs behind her as he spun her around in the air.

"Oh, my God!" she screamed, "I can't believe it's really *you!*" she said so emotionally that a single tear fell from her eye. "I didn't think I'd ever see you again! Oh, my God! How have you been? You look good. You haven't changed one bit!" She rambled until she was out of breath.

"You haven't changed either," he responded. "Damn, baby, I missed you like crazy! I didn't think I'd ever see you again either. But I promise you this: I'll never let you leave out of my life again!" he said surely and they kissed.

He didn't care what kind of life she had before him. He would accept her how she was. He wanted her in his life no matter what. They kissed a kiss that had been long overdue -- one that was kept away by distance, but never left their minds. And when their lips touched and their tongues met, it was just like the very first time. It was the best feeling they'd ever felt in their lives.

"Damn! Well are we going to get introduced?" interrupted Yolanda and Shaylynn.

"Oh, my God, y'all! I'm so sorry!" Davita said as they broke their kiss but stayed wrapped in each other's arms. "Tommy, this is Yolanda and Shaylynn... Yolanda and Shaylynn, this is Tommy... Tommy Good."

"Whass up?" he nodded.

"Fine as you," they flirted.

"Let's order some drinks." Tommy invited them to have a seat at the bar with him and Mike. For the next twenty minutes or so, the five of them got acquainted with one another, but mainly Tommy and Davita got caught up on each other's lives.

Just the two of them in each other's presence for the first time in years had them feeling like giddy middle school students again. They touched each other's hands and face; Patted each other's legs during laughs; Pecked each other on the lips occasionally as they talked, and couldn't wipe the smiles off of their faces. For people standing around watching them it was a sight to see. The two of them must have really been in love. It made some people wish their teenage love were like theirs. Others didn't care one way or another. Some people were jealous and envious, while some people paid them no mind at all. The one thing they did pay attention to was the bar, because they were still ordering drinks compliments of the boy, Tommy Good.

■■■■■■

Hollywood watched the reunion from the V.I.P. and it even made him feel warm inside. The reunion between his sister and Tommy was something special. They must have really made an impact on one another's lives that summer, and they had. Davita had been through the worst times of Tommy's life that summer. It was the summer that he and his boy, Mike found Mike's sister in a Dumpster brutally raped, beaten and murdered. She even went to Michele's funeral, which she sometimes dreamt about. Michele was her friend too.

Hollywood watched as they danced, laughed, kissed, sipped drinks and enjoyed the evening. He couldn't wait to meet the boy, Tommy Good. He had plans -- big plans. Plans that could help him capitalize on another city's drug addiction by pushing his heroin on its street corners. They said Delaware was a gold mine. And the head miner was Tommy Good, his sister's first love. *Jackpot!* he thought. For Hollywood, this meant another soldier on his team.

Chapter Fifteen

I've Been Kissed...
But I Never Knew Love Like This

"**I** see you haven't lost a step," Davita shouted over of the loud music, as they danced to All About The Benjamin's by P. Diddy and the Bad Boy Crew.

"Nah, I see you picked up a few." Tommy was confident of his dance moves and Davita was definitely holding it down.

"I do a little sumptin" – sumptin'," she smiled, and lit up the room.

They were dancing the night away while Mike, Yolanda and Shaylynn were tossing it up at the bar. They loved Mike's sense of humor. He was just as crazy and ghetto as them, but that wasn't all. It was his southern accent they adored.

Mike could tell that Shaylynn was feeling him by the way she was acting, but he decided not to adhere to her advances. At least not right now anyway. He knew if he did that night, he'd never make it home in time for the scheduled appointment to take pictures at Olan Mills studio with Ann and the kids. Ann reminded him before he left out of the house. "Don't forget we're taking pictures tomorrow." And he knew damn well she'd snap if he weren't there. So it was later for Shaylynn. Tonight he was going home.

"Oh shit!" Davita forgot, grabbing Tommy by the hand. "'Come on baby, let me introduce you to my brother."

"Your brother? Who's your brother? I didn't know you had a brother."

"You don't remember I told you I had a brother?"

Tommy tried to reflect if she had or not. "Oh yeah, I remember now but I forget his name."

"Sinqué, but now they call him Hollywood."

"Hollywood?" Tommy pondered. He heard that name several times before.

"Mmm-hmm. Come on let's go."

Davita led and Tommy followed as they left the dance floor. They stopped at the bar to get Mike, Yolanda and Shaylynn first before heading to the V.I.P. where Hollywood was waiting. When they reached the V.I.P. room, Tommy played it calm. They had heard more than enough tales about Hollywood and the way he took care of his business. If they hadn't heard it from so many people and heard tales of how he'd won some major trials in D.C., you would've sworn that Hollywood was a myth.

Tommy and Mike spotted Hollywood as soon as they stepped in the V.I.P. You couldn't miss him. He had the biggest gold chain on his neck with the iciest charm they'd ever seen. And it was original too. Hollywood's charm was a replica of the mountain with the word "Hollywood" written on it. He was dressed in a gold and green Versace shirt with a lion print on it, green slacks and a custom pair of green and gold gator shoes. He looked exactly the way Tommy and Mike imagined him to look, all the way down to the four huge goons that stood around him as he sat.

"Sin..." Davita said to her brother, calling him in a nickname short for Sinqué. She didn't like "Hollywood". He was Hollywood to everybody else. He was "Sin" to her. "...This is Tommy and Mike."

Hollywood stood up to meet them and extended his hand in greetings. He shook Mike's hand first, then took Tommy's and said to the both of them, "I'm glad to finally meet y'all," he finished before sitting back down at the table. "Here, have a seat," he gestured with his hand as more of an order than an offer. Hollywood looked to be in his late twenties, early thirties. He was about 6' 3" or 6' 4", and had a muscular build like he worked out.

"Got-damn! If I ain't know better, I would've thought y'all niggas was try'na outdo me in my city buying the bar out like that," he joked with a smile.

"Nah, it wasn't nothin' like that. I was just playing da game a lil' bit, that's all. Enjoying myself, you feel me?" Tommy replied.

"Yeah, no disrespect was intended," Mike added.

"None was taken, young brothers... none at all. I actually enjoyed it. It was good to see somebody else doing some boss shit for a change."

"I heard that," Tommy responded, and then was interrupted by Davita.

"Okay, that's enough," she said. "Y'all will have plenty of time to talk."

"Alright, Vita! Hold on, damn! It's over in a couple of minutes anyway," Hollywood reminded her.

"That's what I know and I'm ready to go right now! Ain't nobody try'na be caught up in all that traffic try'na get up outta here."

"Where you goin'?" Tommy wanted to follow her.

"Home." Davita hoped he would catch the invite.

"Your crib?" Tommy shot back.

"Oh, that's for sure! That's why I'm tellin' you now that you need to come on!" Davita smiled. She wasn't letting him get far. She had to give him the real deal. When they were younger nothing really jumped off but tonight if he stayed, it was going down.

"Here I come," Tommy said and looked to Hollywood and Mike. "Man, you gon' be straight driving, 'cause you and them broads played the bar close."

"Don't look at me, nigga." Mike kept a straight face before laughing. "Go ahead. I'ma be alright. Just leave me the keys."

"Yeah, go ahead. Me and Mike going to boss it up for a minute. He's in good hands. This is my city and he ain't gotta worry about a mu'fuckin' thing. He wit' Hollywood!" Hollywood reassured Tommy.

"Ai'ight then, Mike, I'ma get wit' chu in the mornin'. Matter fact, call me when you get up."

"Ai'ight."

"And Hollywood, I guess I'll see you whenever."

"Sho'nuff, Tommy Good. I'ma be getting' at you real soon. We need to talk."

"Ai'ight then, I'm out," he shouted as he left with Davita and Shaylynn.

Tommy was glad when they dropped Shaylynn off because from the time they got in Davita's car until the time they stopped at the late night joint for some food, all the way to her doorstep, Shaylynn was talking, and mainly about Mike. Davita confessed later on after they dropped her off that she always does that when she gets drunk -- runs her damn mouth. He made a mental note to monitor her drinking from here on out if they ever went out together again.

Davita pulled up to the guard's tower and flashed a well-mannered smile. "Hello Bob!" she spoke to the old white man. She often wondered what would happen if someone decided to violate the grounds. How would Bob be of any assistance when he looked like Don Knotts from the old show that came on T.V. called "The Andy Griffith Show"? The resemblance made her smile, as did the thought of what Bob would do. She could see him ducking down in the tower if anything happened.

"Hello, Ms. Davita. It's a beautiful night. I see you have company tonight. Is that Tyrone?"

"No it isn't, Bob. When was the last time you saw him around?" she frowned and looked over at Tommy who seemed a little jealous and was all ears.

"I haven't seen him in a long time. The last time I inquired about him you said he was in Europe playing football for the Galaxy. Is that right? Then you said you were expecting him back home, so I kinda figured that was him."

"No, Bob. I'm not with him any more."

"I'm Tommy, your new chum, so get used to seeing me around, okay? I hold good conversations too," Tommy butted in. He was tired of the ongoing Tyrone story. *Fuck Tyrone!* he thought. *My name is Tommy Good!*

"Okay, Tommy. Nice to meet you," Bob warmly greeted him. "Be looking forward to one of them good conversations," and then he lifted the gate.

"You jealous?" Davita asked as she drove under the gate.

"Only when it comes to you," he answered.

"Well, I'm jealous too," she replied.

"When?"

"When it comes to you," she answered, and they smiled.

■■■■■■

Davita led Tommy into her plush two-bedroom apartment. "Excuse the mess." She went straight into the living room and started picking up items. There wasn't much there, just a few out of place magazines on the coffee table. After that, she entered the dining room picking up the curling irons and scissors that were left out when Shaylynn did her hair.

Tommy paid it no attention. He sat down on the couch, grabbed the remote to her flat screen television and began flicking through the channels. He wasn't looking for anything particular but stopped at B.E.T. uncut videos. It was the one Tupac and Jodeci made called "How Do You Want It?" Every time Tommy saw a video of Tupac or heard a song by him, he wondered if the late rapper was really dead. He wondered that because he knew all about Tupac's family history with the Black Panthers. Tupac wasn't just some poor Black kid who happened to luck up on a record deal. He was a poor Black kid who was rich in heritage. He knew who he was, where he came from, and what it meant to be Black in AmeriKKKa. That's why it pained so many people to hear the self-destructive music he made, when his best music was uplifting to the entire Black community as a whole. Songs like:

"Trapped"; "White Man's World"; "Keep Ya Head Up"; "Dear Momma"; "Blasphemy" and all the rest of the songs he made that had some substance to them. That was Tupac at his best. But Tommy couldn't blame him for anything he did wrong because they were two of the same. *Damn, Pac!* Tommy thought as he watched the legend rhyme. Then he turned his attention back to the apartment.

Davita's apartment was nicely decorated. It was very rich in taste and style. The place was painted eggshell-white; the furniture was made of oak wood and expensive leather. A large bookshelf took up one wall of the apartment with books the size of telephone books, and Tommy wondered who would actually want to read a book that size. Then he remembered that she said she was in school to become a podiatrist.

The next thing that caught his eyes were the pictures. There were some on the coffee table and some on the entertainment center where the stereo sat. Then there was a huge one on the wall. Tommy was envious. All those years had passed and Davita shared many memories with another man... and it wasn't him. The pictures were of Davita and Tyrone. One of the pictures looked like they were out at a carnival, another at Kings Dominion in Virginia. Another one of them he assumed to be at some island in the Caribbean. And the biggest picture of them all was of them dressed alike appearing to be very much in love.

"What's wrong, baby?" Davita asked as she flopped down on the couch next to him.

"Am I here to temporary take his place?" He turned his head from side to side peering at all the pictures.

"Awww, that's so cute!" she said and hugged him around the neck. "Baby, don't be jealous. I had to go on with my life. I thought I'd never see you again but you're here now. Tyrone is history! Matter of fact," she said and stood up, "Let me take care of this,' and started grabbing all of the pictures. She removed every last one of them, except the one on the wall because it was too big. Then she put them in her hallway closet. "There. Is that better?"

Tommy had to laugh at the fast elimination of Tyrone.

"I'm surprised one of those fast girls in Delaware hadn't trapped you down, wit' ya' fine ass. You sure did grow to be a handsome ass chocolate man! Mmm, mmm! I'm ready to tear ya ass up!"

"I have plenty of broads chasin' me, but really, I was waiting to bump into you," he gamed her. "Damn baby, I missed the hell outta you. I tried to find someone like you so bad, but it was impossible. You can't be duplicated."

"I'm one of a kind, huh?" she said playfully.

"Nah, baby. I'm dead serious. I wanted to ask Latoya about you so bad."

"Why didn't you?"

"Because I thought you probably didn't remember me or would have forgotten all about what we had as kids. Feel me? I imagined you would've thought I was stalkin' you or something."

"It wouldn't have been stalking. Actually, I was kind of feeling the same way."

"Well, why didn't you ask about me?"

"Probably because I felt the same way you did. Tommy, I still can't believe you're here. Do you feel the same way? It's crazy for me, because I kinda wished you back. I thought of all the things we could do together. There would be no restraints or limits to what we could do. We're grown now. No more Aunt Cookie or Big Mom."

"You remember Big Mom?"

"Yeah. How can I forget? Remember the days at her house? How we used to try and sneak and do the nasty but couldn't because somebody was always home... or they'd walk in? Or we'd be just too scared? Do you remember that?"

"Yeah, I remember that. I remember those days like it was yesterday," Tommy played back his memory.

"Well, are you just going to sit there, or are you going to kiss me? Or do I gotta put my tongue in your mouth again like I had to do at Aunt Cookie's that night?" she teased.

"Oh, shit done changed since then, baby girl," Tommy warned, and slid closer to her.

"I'm glad to know that."

Tommy grabbed Davita around the waist and the two of them kissed passionately. What started out soft and mellow became animalistic within seconds. There was no way for them to hold back the built up lust they had carried around for years for one another. Both dreamed for this moment and it had finally come -- the moment they'd been waiting for. Tommy and Davita grabbed at each other's clothes, fondled with each other's body parts, then rolled to the floor. Davita straddled Tommy as he laid flat on his back with her Coogi dress hiked up around her satin thighs, and Tommy let his hands find them. Frustrated with trying to unbutton his shirt, she grabbed it on both sides and yanked it open. Buttons flew everywhere. That turned her on even more. Davita leaned down and kissed his chest, working her way to his neck, then let her lips find his again.

Tommy was rock hard and knew she could feel it pressing up against her inner-thighs through the fabric of his pants. He let his hands slide up her thighs until he had two hands full of her ass and caressed it softly. With each squeeze he scooted her dress up even higher until her bare ass covered only by a thong, was exposed to the cool air of the room temperature. *"Smack!"* Tommy slapped that ass and she jumped.

"Mmmm!" she moaned in his ear before letting her tongue find his earlobe. He squirmed and then sat up so they were facing each other. Davita lifted her arms straight up in the air and Tommy lifted her dress over her head. Her body was perfect and unblemished. The red matching bra and thong set she wore complimented her skin-tone to a tee. It looked so good on her body that he didn't want to take it off so he left it on. He just lifted her bra to reveal her breasts and sucked and nibbled on her sweet brown nipples. "Sssss!" she sucked air through her teeth as she tugged at his belt.

"Baby take your pants off," she whined and started rubbing her own titties as Tommy removed his pants. "Hurry up, baby!" she encouraged him as if he was moving too slowly.

"I'm trying, baby," he said, finally getting his pants off down around his knees. He flicked them across the room with his foot right at the picture on the wall. And just what he intended to happen, happened. The picture fell off the wall and slid behind the loveseat. They both laughed.

"He was staring at my ass," Tommy joked.

"Boy, you so crazy!"

Tommy rolled Davita over as they lay in between the couch and the coffee table. He put both of her legs up -- one on the couch and the other on the coffee table. Then he went face first. Davita arched her back until her ass was off the rug when Tommy slid his fingers inside of her. She was soaking wet. Tommy flicked his tongue in and out of her body while his thumbs held her open, causing her love button to pop out like a pinky tip. He swirled the little piece of meat around in his mouth sending chills through her body as her legs shook uncontrollably and she tried to run.

"Mmm-mmm!" he said, and wrapped his arms around her waist so she couldn't move while he continued to eat her out. The feeling felt so good that she couldn't hold it back any longer. The scream of joy came from the pit of her stomach as she exploded into an orgasm. Tommy knew she had cum because he could taste the coating on his tongue. He savored the flavor with a few smacks of his lips and then turned her ass over. From the back, Tommy pulled her thong to the side and entered her body from the rear. Her pussy was tight, warm and wet, fitting him like a glove.

"Oh my God!" she moaned to the pleasure of him stroking her from behind. "Oh my God!" she moaned again. *"Oooooo,* baby, yeah! Right there! Don't! Stop! *Oooooo,* yeah baby!" she continued as she ran her fingers through the rug and Tommy stroked faster. "Ooooo, baby, *Oh my God!* I'm cumming!" she screamed. "I'm cumming again!" she said, and her body shuttered as they came together.

Davita was exhausted. So was Tommy. He collapsed on the floor right beside her and the two of them were lost in the same thought as they stared up at the ceiling.

There's not anything in the world like your first-love. They only come once in a lifetime.

Chapter Sixteen

The Heroin Connect - 1998

Tommy and Mike had stayed up nearly half the night debating and going over some numbers. They had talked to several niggas around the way who had crossed over into the heroin field and gave them the inside scoop.

"Man, we tripled our money in weeks! That's why we haven't been buying weight from y'all lately. You got some cheap numbers on a heroin connect," the younger hustler informed.

"That's what y'all need to do is start selling weight in dope. Y'all already got the coke on lock. If y'all do that, y'all can sew up the game on both ends. Feel me?" one of their used-to-be big spenders said.

And it made a lot of sense. *Why not kill 'em from every angle?* was the thought they had, and by the end of the night they came to a conclusion: They were going to call Hollywood.

Tommy pulled out his cell and called Hollywood. Since it was still early, he figured they could sit down over lunch and discuss some prices with him, while at the same time have Hollywood familiarize him with everything about the dope game. How to cut the dope? What to use to cut the dope? Will the dope go bad? What's the best way to move the dope? All those questions he needed to be taught from square one.

"What's up Tommy Good?" Hollywood answered, seeing it was his newfound brother-in-law by the number on his cellphone screen.

"Whass' up wit' you?"

"Ain't nothin', Jo."

"I'm trying to sit down and talk to you about some numbers."

"About time. Where you at?"

"I'm just now leaving Vita's spot."

"Oh, so you in B-more?"

"Yeah."

"Well look, meet me down at the Harbor then. That way we can grab somethin' to eat. Plus, I gotta come to B-more anyway. I gotta check some shit out down in the Murphy Homes."

"Murphy Homes?"

"Yeah, that's the projects."

"Oh, so you down in the projects now?" Tommy pried.

"Yeah, I took your advice. I need to have my ears to the streets. I'm down here in the southeast. Yo, Jo, I ain't know how much outta touch I was until I got down here, Jo. I don't know nobody out this mu'fucka! Made a nigga appreciate shit and get a new hunger for some more shit."

"I told you, nigga. That's why I stay in da 'hood. Yeah, I moved from out of da 'hood but I ain't going nowhere, feel me? That's how I stay grounded."

"I heard that, Jo. Well look, I'm fitt'n to get up outta here and come your way. So meet me down at the Harbor in about an hour and a half."

"Ai'ight, I'll be there," Tommy promised, and hung up the phone.

■■■■■■

In the late 1960's, early 1970's, as men came back to AmeriKKKan soil from the Vietnam War, 80% of them were strung out on heroin. It was a drug made from poppy seeds to take away pain from gunshot wounds. It was also used as a drug to numb the consciousness of the men who carried the automatic weapons. It made them have no feelings or regards to whom or whatever they decided to kill. Then as the war ended and the men returned home, they returned home with drug habits. They yearned for the drug that they were fed over in Vietnam, physically and mentally. They needed the drug to function; needed the drug to take away the feeling they felt inside when they flashed back on a time when they had to murder a person -- man, woman or child.

The U.S. government claimed they had no idea that the drug was so addictive. Many people found that hard to believe. They knew exactly what they were doing. They were creating another epidemic for the Black community. It's easy to believe these facts because out of the 80% that came back addicted to the drug, 75% of them were Black. There was a conspiracy -- a Black conspiracy, and heroin began killing the low-level economic communities.

Once they did find out just how addictive the drug was they put it on the market for sale. The "catch 22" was that it was considered an illegal, uncontrolled substance -- a narcotic. Either you were going to become addicted to the drug as a user, or you were going to jail as a dealer. The Black community was in trouble.

As for the addicted individuals, they were hooked on another drug called methadone. Then in the 80's crack came along and took over the heroin epidemic. It almost became non-existent, but now it was back. In 1998, heroin was back and taking over once again. This time it targeted people as a whole. It swept through the Black and white communities, and people were calling it the drug of the new millennium.

Tommy and Mike knew why they weren't making as much money or moving as much cocaine as they used to. They were still moving at the least 8 kilos a week. But just a few months ago, they were doing at least 12 kilos a week. They had heard about the dope game and how it was making a comeback and strongly considered it. Hollywood kept trying to tell them about the dope game since that's all he fucked with in D.C.

"I'm tellin' y'all, y'all need to come and take some of this dope off my hands," he would say to them.

Hollywood had plenty of heroin. He was dealing with a major Mexican cartel that was dropping pounds and pounds of "Mexican mud" on him monthly. He built his organization up on pure muscle in the D.C. He was rich, not wealthy. He was easily bringing in a million or better profits a week from D.C. to New York. And he told Tommy and Mike on more than one occasion that he could promise them triple the money they were seeing in a month's time. At first they didn't cross over, but decided quickly they had to. Heroin was taking over. They wouldn't have a choice but to bow down if they wanted to keep doing major numbers.

■■■■■■

Hollywood drove his Italian-made Pagani Zonda across the city of D.C., headed over to the southeast side. He stopped at a red light on L Street and mashed the gas as he sat in neutral.

'This is why I bought this car, 'cause this mu'fucka got power! Listen to that," he spoke to his passenger, Lil' Shawn, as the $370,000 machine barked, howled and roared to life.

Hollywood looked at the white man in the car that pulled up on the side of him and smiled. He knew why the man was looking at him like "that". He was trying to figure out how a young Black man could afford a car like the one he was driving, a question that would go unanswered, because as soon as the light turned green, Hollywood sped off leaving the man two street lights behind.

"Fuckin' nigger!" the white man cursed.

Hollywood continued towards southeast to the projects they called "Little Beirut". Earning its name for all the gunplay and violence that embarked its community. Little Beirut was the most dangerous housing ghetto on that side of town and one of Hollywood's main drug spots.

"Lil' Shawn," Hollywood said as they neared the war zone, "Call them niggas and let 'em know we almost there. I want them niggas on point."

"Ai'ight, Jo. I'ma do that right now," Lil' Shawn replied and pulled out his cellphone. "Yeah, whass'up, Jo? Yeah, dis Lil' Shawn. Look man, we right around the corner, so y'all niggaz need to be on point. Yeah, we coming right now, Jo," he said and hung up the phone.

"Is everything cool?"

"Come on now, Hollywood, you know my team is nothing less than the best, Jo," Lil' Shawn assured.

Lil' Shawn was the same age as Hollywood. They grew up together in the D.C. streets, but they were direct opposites. Hollywood was a hustler, while Lil' Shawn was a young gun. While Hollywood was going hand-to-hand on the street corners, Lil' Shawn was putting bullets in niggas for the cash. All you had to do was get a Polaroid of the nigga you wanted done in and you could call it a wrap because three days later, they'd be in the obituary section of the newspaper. Lil' Shawn was an assassin. Hollywood hired him the moment he got on with the Mexicans and he'd been with him ever since. He was the head of Hollywood's security, and just in this year alone, he had accounted for many bodies.

When they turned into the entrance of little Beirut, Lil' Shawn glanced on both sides of the street. "What I tell you, Jo," he said to Hollywood as two men with microphone headset walkie-talkies lead them with a hand gesture.

"I know that's right!" Hollywood said, impressed by the surveillance.

The surveillance team had just been added as part of the program. There had been too many busts by the D.C. Police Department and Hollywood was getting frustrated. And they were taking dealers off the streets too. Just last month they got one of the three houses for two kilos of the brown stone called pure heroin. So Hollywood set out to fix the problem by adding the surveillance to the entire neighborhood, which gave the dealers and the drug houses a heads up on the police before they could reach them. So by the time they did raid, the drugs would have already been transferred somewhere else. And it was working up to this point. There were no successful raids, no street corner busts.

Hollywood pulled his car over and parked in front of the building where his work was being moved. This was his first time out on the streets in a minute, but it looked the same. It still gave him that feeling, that rush, the hunger to want more out of life for him and his family. He looked out his windshield at the mess some called life and watched time pass.

Trash littered the lawns, little kids in tattered clothes ran in and out the alleyways unattended. Their parents were probably one of these men or women out there zombified or comatose on drugs. Old, used syringes and their orange tops decorated the gutters, and prostitutes lined the street turning the block into a hoe-stroll.

Hollywood shook his head in shame. This is what made him want out of the ghetto as a child. There was no way he was going to continue living the way he was living. His childhood wasn't as bad as some of these kids' because his mother didn't use drugs, but times were still rough. He hated seeing his mother pull long hours at two jobs, then come home exhausted, barely able to keep her eyes open to tend to him and Davita. He would often tell his mom on the days she came in tired like that, that one day he was going to take care of her and that she wouldn't have to work any more. That day had come, because now she was the proud owner of Davita Sinque's Soul Food Restaurant, named after her kids.

Davita Sinque's was Chocolate City's number one soul food restaurant. It rang bells in people's ears all over and was a major tourist attraction to visitors of the nation's capitol. Some of the other names mentioned with it were: Sylvia's in Harlem, Roscoe's in California, and Gladys Knight's Chicken & Waffles in Atlanta. Hollywood was proud of each and every accomplishment that he was able to achieve.

Now, as he sat smack dead in the middle of the ghetto, he was glad that he took Tommy's advice. He was in the ghetto not to drop drugs off, because he had someone to do that. He wasn't in the ghetto to collect money, because he had someone to do that too. He was in the ghetto because he lost touch with where he came from, and he was reminded of just how much he was out of touch the longer he sat there.

"Yo, I got some business to take care of with Tommy Good. Let's go handle that," Hollywood instructed Lil' Shawn and went to meet with Tommy Good.

■■■■■■

Tommy jumped in his new Lexus LS450 and headed down to the Harbor to meet Hollywood. He parked in a parking lot owned by a private owner and gave the man at the booth his keys. The man in return, handed Tommy a ticket and gave the keys to his co-worker, who jumped behind the wheel of Tommy's car to park it in the lot.

Tommy walked down towards the Harbor and saw all the people down around the water, and he realized why he loved the Harbor so much. He loved it because it gave him peace. Just seeing the happy couples holding hands, laughing, enjoying life together and all the activities of the Harbor made him feel good. The aquarium, the E.S.P.N. Zone, the Science Center, the restaurants and everything else about the Harbor was a reminder of the joys of life. It was also an escape from the reality he was living in.

For the people visiting, it was a temporary escape. Then they had to go back to the same reality they left from. Back to slaving at the job for 40 hours a week, back to the housing projects or Section 8 house that a lot of us were accustomed to. Back to the spouse that you were cheating on with your jump-off, the one you wanted to leave but the one you were scared to leave because you knew deep down inside that that person was the one who loved you.

Just seeing life for what it was was good, and that's what the Harbor did for Tommy. It reminded him that life was complicated and wasn't just some walk in the park. It reminded him that he needed to find out what made him happy in life and being content was a major must on his list.

Hollywood chose the Rusty Scupper restaurant as the place to meet. It was probably the most popular restaurant at the Harbor. It actually sat on the water. It served the regular menu of steak and seafood lunches and dinners, and that's what Hollywood had a taste for today. A nice steak, lobster tail and some crab claws.

Tommy walked into the restaurant and saw Hollywood at a table with a river view. He was sitting there with Lil' Shawn. Tommy knew that Lil' Shawn was his gun, but he didn't fear him at all. The eyes don't lie and Tommy knew he was not who he portrayed to be. Yeah, without a doubt, Lil' Shawn was an assassin and he'd shoot in a heartbeat if given the order. But he wasn't a cold-blooded killer. Tommy knew what a killer's eyes looked like, because he looked into them every day when he looked at his other half. Mike was a cold-blooded killer.

Tommy greeted the both of them and kind of gave Lil' Shawn a smirk before he sat down. He was still thinking about his eyes and how he's up here right now trying to portray like some real hard mu'fucka. Lil' Shawn was soft. He was soft as funeral music inside and didn't understand why Hollywood couldn't see it. *I wonder why Hollywood don't see that shit,* Tommy thought to himself, but left well enough alone. It wasn't his problem, it was Hollywood's. And just in case him and Mike decided to use "Plan B", he knew just who to go after -- *This pussy right here,* he thought.

Tommy and Hollywood threw numbers back and forth across the table as they ate lunch, going over the dos and don'ts of the dope game, while trying to come up with a reasonable number. Sixty dollars a gram would be the price they settled on and Hollywood would give him pure "Mexican Mud."

"The dope is so good," Hollywood told him, "It could stand a five cut."

That meant that every gram be bought could stand five grams of cut and still be good. If he decided to put a three on it, the dope could knock a nigga on his ass. It almost seemed too good to be true, but it was for real. That was the difference between the dope game and the coke game. With the dope,- you could triple your money at the least but it also bought along a whole bunch of heat. That was because people needed the dope. They would actually hunt you down for the drug and that's what brought along the police. Tommy wouldn't have to worry about that though, because he wouldn't be going hand-to-hand. He would only be dealing with the dealers but he had to watch out for them too. Keep his ear to the street and make sure that the niggas coming to cop from him was on the up and up and not cased up with some open charges and shit. That's what he had to do. After he was sure about the move he was ready to make, him and Hollywood made the deal. Tommy was going to make a trial run with the dope first, only buying a kilo. Then he'd move onto the larger quantities if it progressed.

Once the conversation was over, Tommy was ready to get started. That began his business in the dope game.

Chapter Seventeen

Let's Get Married

Tommy rolled over and smiled at the sight of his sleeping beauty when he woke up in the morning. It wasn't a better feeling in the world for a man than to wake up and see something beautiful lying next to his side. Six months had passed and Tommy got that luxury mostly every single day. They rotated living arrangements. Today was a special day though. It was a day that marked their six-month reunion together and he planned something special for the weekend but first, he needed to talk to Hollywood.

"Good morning Beauty," Tommy acknowledged and kissed her on the forehead.

"Good morning. Where you think you goin'?" she asked, as Tommy sat on the side of the bed putting his clothes on. "Today is our six month anniversary back together."

"I know that, baby. That's why I got something planned for the weekend - something real special," he said with a smile.

"What?"

"It wouldn't be special if I told you."

"Yes it would 'cause then I'd have something to look forward to."

"I'm not telling you, so stop asking. Just know you're going to love it."

"So where you going?"

"I'm about to call Sinque, I mean Hollywood."

"You said his name right the first time."

"Well, you know what I mean. I'm about to call your brother. I gotta sit down and talk to him about something," he answered before standing up and heading towards the bathroom.

Davita wanted to say something to Tommy about it, but decided against it. She knew what talking to her brother meant and she didn't like it. Besides, it probably would've only started an argument. She had already told Tommy more than once to stop associating himself with Sinque because it could be dangerous. She loved him to death but she knew who and what her brother was about. He was "Hollywood" -- a marked man. Marked nearly by everyone from the police to the feds down in Quantico. The stick-up boys, rival drug dealers trying to take over his spot as the boss and the big man on the campus of the "School of Hard Knocks". She knew it was only a matter of time before one of them got to him. She knew he wouldn't be alive much longer or in jail for the rest of his life. That's why she tried to mentally and spiritually prepare for the inevitable. It would be just too much to lose Tommy too.

"Baby," she said, when he returned from the bathroom, "What do you have to talk to Sinque about?"

"About this weekend," he lied. "He's supposed to be helping me get something for you."

"Yeah, right. Nice try. You think I got 'stupid' written across my forehead?" she cynically stated, but he didn't reply. He just grabbed his keys and gave her a kiss on the lips.

"Yo, stop worrying yourself so much. I'll talk to you later," he tried to comfort her.

■■■■■■

"What about this ring right here?" Tommy asked for Hollywood's assistance. He knew he didn't want anything but he best for his sister. He showed him a $25,000 H colored diamond ring.

"That's it right there, playa!" Hollywood gave his approval.

What better time than now? Tommy thought as he pictured asking Davita to marry him.

After he purchased the ring, Hollywood went about his business and so did Tommy. His business with Hollywood was about to come to an abrupt end.

■■■■■■

"Why da fuck we wanna keep dealing with Hollywood?" Tommy blasted on Mike.

Over the last six months they learned all they needed to learn about dope game. Tommy didn't want to deal through Hollywood anymore. He wanted the straight connection.

"We need the connect ourselves and if the nigga don't give it to us, then, well, you know..." he said to Mike. "We move onto Plan B."

The love Tommy shared with his future wife was true but for Hollywood it was nothing more than game. A true hustler recognized that, as did Tommy. Mike laughed because he knew what Plan B meant. "Yeah, plan B... Plan B has always been my favorite," Mike concluded.

To

"CLASSY"

Chapter Eighteen

The Classy Years - 2005
Seven Years Later...

It was amazing how a few good business moves, a couple of good choices, having a beautiful wife and kids and seven years could change your life. He married his childhood sweetheart in a beautiful ceremony and brought her back to the place they met - Wilmington, Delaware.

It was also amazing how bad your conscious could make you feel about some of the moves you made. All in all though, you had to decide on two things -- either you were going to let your conscious eat at you or you were going to come to terms with who you were -- be alright with the choices you made. Understand why you made them. And what caused you to make them in the first place. Tommy was cool with them all.

However, there were times when his conscious ate at him but he always found a way to escape the memories. His favorite, just looking around him and taking inventory of the things he had, and understanding that none of it would have been possible had he not made the choices he made.

Tommy drove his favorite toy, a black on black convertible Bentley, smoothly down his city's 9th Street. Tommy was a 'hood legend on the city's east side section, and throughout Delaware for that matter, as was Mike. They had singlehandedly put the state of Delaware, a state barely visible on the map, onto the tongues of nearly every person's mouth that was in the streets. It was that serious. Tommy and Mike set the standard. Tommy continued down 9th Street slowly. He tooted his horn as he rode past C.B.W. (Clifford Brown Walk) at the niggas who were standing outside on the corners, then flashed a smile and a wink at the young girls who instantly turned to mush, as Mike Jones' "Back Then" pounded through the speakers. He was "Tommy Good"! All the doe boys that were trying to become somebody tried to pattern themselves after him and Mike.

Tommy pulled up to the corner of 9th and Pine Street and made a left, headed towards 10th Street. Tenth and Pine was where it was happening. And as usual the block was packed with people running in and out of the Indian's little corner store or niggas flagging people down who looked to be potential customers. Tenth Street was a gold mine.

Tommy pulled his Bentley over to the curb in front of the store and got out to run inside. This was one of his rituals -- one he picked up from Uncle Bear -- to go in the store and grab up a newspaper and an orange juice. He did this at first just to read the local section. But now it was business. He was mainly concerned with the stock market section of the paper. He liked to keep up on his money, the money he wisely invested in all the right companies thanks to his brother Marcus, who had become a stockbroker.

They hadn't been close in years. Marcus knew his brother's lifestyle and didn't want any parts of it until he decided the way to help Tommy was to help him make legal money in the event that things didn't work out. At first Tommy was skeptical about investing his money in places where he had no control over it. But when Marcus broke it down to him, he understood the game.

"Look, Tommy," Marcus began. "Now you know I wouldn't tell you anything wrong. The stock market is like the game; only white people tend to play it. I mean, Black people are starting to buy into the game of stocks, but most are scared to take the chance. We're just really starting to catch on. Anyway, here's how it goes:

You buy into companies with things called 'shares' and then you monitor them carefully. It's sorta like the saying in poker.

You gotta know when to hold them, know when to fold them. Only thing with stocks is you gotta know when to buy them, know when to sell them. Meaning that, if you buy a share at two dollars apiece and overnight they shoot up to twelve dollars apiece, you have a decision to make. That's where the gamble begins. Do you keep them or do you sell them? If you move wisely you'll become a very wealthy man. If you move cautiously or scared, chances are you'll lose money." He told his brother, and Tommy bought into it. It was a hustle. You bought and flipped shares legally in a game called the "stock market". And since Tommy knew he was a born hustler, he figured, *how can I lose?* And his intuitions were right. He and his little brother became vigorous in a game made for the *other man*.

A recent graduate of Morehouse College in Atlanta, Marcus had become one of the most sought after brothas in the business and he was only twenty-three years old, while his brother, Tommy was on the verge of retiring from the game -- the streets.

Tommy came out of the store carrying the newspaper under his arm while he sipped his orange juice. He stopped and stood on the corner to bust it up with some young boys who had surrounded his car because that's what kept him grounded. After he did the regular, he told them to stay in school, hit the books and be good. He handed each one of them a ten-dollar bill.

He got back behind the wheel of his car and pulled away from the curb, headed in no particular direction. He was just zoning out. The young boys were still fresh on his mind. He thought about why he still dibbled and dabbled in the game that went against everything he tried so hard to accomplish, but couldn't come up with an answer.

Davita had told him after the surprisingly devastating murder of her beloved brother, to give up the game, but he didn't, and he wasn't.

Life had changed for Davita drastically. It didn't matter for Tommy; he lost his Uncle Bear to the game. He'd just found out his mother was H.I.V. positive. None of that mattered though. Death surrounded him. Tommy had already made up his mind that he was going to die in the streets. It was his destiny and he was going to ride it until the wheels fell off.

He did however manage to come up with another idea though, one that would put him on the backburner and take him out of the spotlight for a while. He needed some young boys on his team who were just as hungry as him and Mike to get money. And he had just the three in mind:

The boy, Zyaire from the Hilltop they called "Zy" for short; The boy, Boomer from 24th Street; and the boy Peacock. Those were the three names that were ringing bells in the streets and Tommy had done his homework. What he gathered on the three was that they met each other in jail sometime last year. Since then they had all been released and hooked up together on the outside. They pumped a little coke on 24th and Carter, moved a little dope up on Market Street and even dabbled in a little bit of weed, but it was really nothing major. They were just maintaining.

Tommy knew how it was to be juggling. He knew from experience what the young boys were going through. He also knew from experience that if they ever wanted to see some real money, they were going to have to get grimy. Just hustling wasn't going to work.

Tommy remembered times they would sell as little of a half-ounce of coke to somebody, and Mike would go and rob the person back for it. When the person came back and told Tommy about it he would just say, "Don't worry about it," and then front them the same half-ounce back. Now the person owed him $350. Then there were the times they simply had to kill a mutha'fucka. Make a nigga come up missing just to prove a point. That's how they came up in the game. And Tommy knew Zy, Boomer and Peacock were willing to go there.

Another way to come up was to have a blazin' connect. That's where Tommy was going to come in. He figured that if he and Mike started dropping bricks of coke and dope off to them, it would free up some time in their personal lives. Tommy would be able to keep a steady eye on the market, spend quality time with his family and travel the globe.

Tommy drove his Bentley across the Market Street Bridge and continued to 24th Street, the area they called "turf". He turned on 23rd Street and drove down to Carter Street and made a left and then parked.

■■■■■■

Zy, Boomer and Peacock were sitting on the step in front of Aunt Cat's house. It was blazing hot outside, so they were dressed in jean shorts and tank tops, while Boomer was shirtless. There wasn't any money coming in all today, just a couple of dollars here and there. When it was like this outside, all they did was plot and plan on a come-up, and today wasn't any different. The seesaw they were riding on was beginning to get discouraging and they needed to make something happen. Flipping the same 4-½ ounces, then having to bust it down in three ways wasn't adding up right. Something had to give.

"Fuck this shit, man! I'ma bout to rob me a mu'fucka!" Peacock said, breaking the silence.

"I been was thinkin' 'bout that," Zy added.

"Well why y'all two mu'fuckas just sayin' something?" Boomer asked. He was the wildest of the three.

"Because, nigga, we was on some ole let's just grind the honest way... don't draw no focus on ourselves bullshit. But fuck dat! It's time to get some real paper," Peacock said, getting excited.

"Man, ain't nothin' honest about this game," Boomer said.

"I bet'cha Tommy and Mike ain't get it the honest way," Zy added, bringing up their two role models.

"Hell no them niggaz ain't get it honest!" Peacock said. "I remember when I was a young boy, and me and my mom lived up on 27th Street. We watched them throw some dude in the trunk! Yo, it was shovels and all kinda shit back there. Yo, ain't nobody seen dat nigga yet!"

"Word?" Zy asked.

"Word, nigga!"

"I think I know who you talkin' 'bout, Peacock. You talkin' 'bout the boys Oscar and Shawn!"

"Yeah, I think that was their names. How you know that? You heard that too?" Peacock asked Boomer.

"Yeah, I heard it from my Aunt Butter one night. You know they used to mess around, right?"

"Ya Aunt who? Butter?" Peacock curiously questioned.

"Yeah, Butter," Boomer responded.

'Duck Butter? The one that run the massage parlor?' Peacock was shocked.

'Yeah, nigga! That's Tommy shit. My Aunt just run dat shit."

"D-a-a-a-m!" Peacock called out, dragging the word out in an envious type of way. "I wish I was Tommy," he said, thinking about all that ass Duck Butter had.

"Fuck you, nigga! Anyway, I heard her talking to her girls one time. She said that niggaz knew it was Tommy and Mike who was making niggaz come up missing, but niggaz is so shook of 'em they scared to say somethin'," Boomer said.

"Niggaz is still shook," Peacock added as Tommy rounded the corner. "And that was like ten years ago."

"Yo! There go Tommy right there!" Zy said as they watched him get out of the Bentley.

Tommy got out of his car and walked over to where the young boys five years his junior was sitting on the steps. He greeted them with a pound of the fist, and they admired the Rolex that hung loosely on his wrist.

"Whass good, lil' niggaz? What 'chall out here doin'?" Tommy asked as he stood on the curb before them.

"Just chillin'. Tryin' to get a coupla dollaz, that's all," Zy spoke up.

"I know that's right! Ain't a mu'fuckin' thing wrong wit' dat. So what, y'all hustlin' right now?"

"Yeah, but ain't no money comin'," Boomer replied.

"I guess not!" Tommy responded like he was about to say something they already knew. "What y'all expect? I see why ain't no money comin'. It's like forty niggaz out here pumpin' in a four-block radius and all y'all pumpin' the same shit. You ain't never gonna see no money that way. Y'all gotta start selling that shit to them, feel me? Y'all gotta start selling some weight around this mutha'fucka."

"Tommy, man, we ain't built like that," Peacock said honestly.

"That's why I'm here," he said, and then turned to Boomer. "I was talkin to your Aunt Butter last night about you niggaz. She said y'all might be able to help me out. And from the way shit is lookin' right now and from what y'all is tellin' me, it looks like I'ma be helpin' y'all out alot more than y'all helpin' me out. So whass'up? Y'all tryin' to holla at a nigga or what? 'Cause I know it's a whole lotta niggaz out there that would love to jump on this opportunity. I'm coming at y'all 'cause y'all my little niggaz. I like you little niggaz. I've had my eye on y'all for a minute now," he said. "So whass'up? Y'all comin' to talk or not? If so, go put dat shit up. Don't get in my car dirty."

Zy, Boomer and Peacock looked at each other in disbelief. It seemed too good to be true. Less than five minutes ago they were sitting on the step bitchin' about how they needed some money and how fucked up it felt to be broke, who they were going to stick-up and when they were going to do it. Now they were being offered the opportunity of a lifetime to get on the team with Tommy Good and Mike. The question now was what was he offering? They knew once they got in the car with Tommy and made a commitment to whatever it was he was offering, there was no turning back. They knew whatever it was it would be a come-up, but they also knew that there were no mistakes allowed. That's what was so scary about the whole situation. They knew that Tommy and Mike wouldn't hesitate to do something to them when it came down to business. But they knew they wouldn't let anything happen to them either. They were strictly business when it came to work, but they played when it came time to play. So that made the decision even easier for them. Who wouldn't want to play on Tommy's team?

Tommy waited for Zy to stash the package behind the row houses that they were pumping in front of, while Boomer and Peacock got in the car with him. His plan was to give them the rundown on what he wanted to put together and see if they were with it or not. He couldn't lose no matter how he went about it, because all the work he had, he got it for free.

So why not look into it, youngins? he thought, as Zy jumped in the car behind Peacock, who was in the front passenger seat.

Tommy drove up Carter Street and made a left onto 24th Street and headed slowly up the block. With the top down on the Bentley, he made sure everyone seen who was in the car with him. He did that because he didn't want any of these niggaz to get the wrong idea or think of doing something stupid to them when they locked thecity down.

"Whass good, nigga?" Tommy yelled out of the convertible to his cousin Sly D, as Sly D jumped out his BMW wagon.

"Whass good wit' chu, cousin?" Sly D asked, lighting a Dutchie.

"Ain't nuffin'. Just came through to snatch up my youngins, you know?'" he said, and they all nodded their heads at Sly D.

"Whass'up, y'all lil' niggaz?" Sly D said before turning the conversation back to Tommy. "Yo, whass'up though? How Big Mom doin'? Is she ai'ight?"

"Big Mom is still doin' what she do. I just dropped some stacks on her to get her kitchen remodeled. You know she ain't moving nowhere. She's the brick that keeps the family together. Nigga, you know, Your pops still living with her. Some things

146

ain't never gon' change... and neither is Big Mom. You better get 'cha ass over to see her. She ain't getting' no younger."

"I heard that. You seen my Pop lately?" he asked, and Tommy couldn't do nothing but laugh. "Whass funny, nigga?"

"Yeah nigga, I'm looking at him. You funny looking ass nigga. You look just like your Pop," Tommy teased, looking at the younger version of his Uncle Willie.

"I know that shit it crazy, right?" Sly D responded, and then the car behind them blew the horn.

Tommy turned around and looked back out the rear of the convertible with his murder-one grit on. He couldn't believe a nigga disrespected him like that in his city. These are my mu'fuckin' streets! "I'll do what I want and when I want in these mu'fuckas! he said to himself." He was just about to open his door and get out to go check the nigga in the car behind him, but he hadn't moved fast enough. Boomer had already leaped from the back seat over the side of the car like it was a fence, and was headed to the car behind them.

"Nigga, what da fuck is yo' problem?" Boomer yelled at the dude in the car, but his windows were rolled up.

The guy was shaking like a leaf as Boomer barked at him from behind the windows. His initial thought was to back up down the street, but there were cars behind him. He looked over at his girl, embarrassed that he was being punked right in front of her and she just rolled her eyes. *A faggot-ass nigga!* she thought to herself as she saw the fear in his eyes. *I told him not to blow the horn.* She knew who was in the car and tried to tell him, but he wanted to be hard. "Fuck Tommy!" he had said, and now he had to deal with it.

"I don't know what 'chu lookin' at me for! He's talkin' to *you!*" she said harshly.

"Nigga, I said what da fuck is yo' problem!" Boomer said, getting angrier as everyone looked on. They knew he was a loose cannon, that's why they didn't go anywhere. They wanted to see what he was going to do. There was no telling with Boomer though, 'cause he was as unpredictable as the weather.

Boomer felt the eyes on him and he knew now that he was forced to set an example. "Nigga, I said what da fuck is yo' problem!" he snapped. Boomer punched straight through the window. "Nigga, you gon' say somethin'!" he said, and smacked him viciously as he dragged him out the driver-side window. He then snatched the 9mm he had in the small of his back out so fast that people didn't even see it. All they saw was the damage it was doing with each swing.

His girl jumped out of the car to safety as she watched from the sidewalk. She couldn't believe her man was a bitch-ass nigga. Yeah, she understood the dude had a gun, but that wasn't it. It was the way he looked at her. She saw straight through all that gangsta shit he played. And she knew from that very moment that she'd never look at him the same. *And that nigga got a nerve to hit on me!* she thought before saying, "Dat's right! Beat his punk ass!" and walked off down the street. When the people looking on heard that, they all started laughing.

"Alright, lil' nigga, that's enough! Come on, let's go," Tommy commanded, and Boomer left the guy lying in the middle of the street. Tommy smiled. *This little nigga is a live-wire*, he thought, and they were off to a good start. He liked Boomer's style. He was intimidating. He could tell by the way people were looking at him while he pistol-whipped the dude.

"Alright, cousin," Tommy said when Boomer got back in the car. "Let me get up outta here."

"Alright, nigga. Holla at me," Sly D replied and watched as his cousin pulled off.

"Nigga's in trouble now!"

Chapter Nineteen

The Drop Off

Tommy drove around the city of Wilmington with the same motive he had when he was on the north side; To let everyone see who he was riding with. He stopped on every major drug corner, every hangout and every set to make sure their faces would be remembered because they were the ones who were about to be running the city. Tommy had enough cocaine and heroin to last for almost a year. Even if Boomer, Zy and Peacock sold a brick of each drug apiece, they still wouldn't run out.

Tommy and Mike had made so much money in the stock market that they really didn't need to sell drugs. But since they had it, they wanted to move it. They were in possession of one hundred bricks of cocaine that they were going to let the young boys have on consignment at $14,500 apiece, which would approximately bring them in $1.5 million. They also had fifty bricks of heroin, which sold at around $80 a gram; that equaled out to about $80,000 a brick. He planned on giving them to Zy, Boomer and Peacock for a little under $70 a gram, and charging them only $65,000 a brick. That would bring in about $3.3 million, putting them at a cool $2.4 million apiece to split. It couldn't have worked out better for them, being as though they hadn't spent a dime to get it.

Tommy drove around for almost two hours talking to Zy, Boomer and Peacock about the game. He told them that they needed to be hungry and stay hungry. Don't let a little bit of money go to their heads.

"Yo," he began. "Dont limit yourselves to nothin'. It's never a limit. Y'all can go as far as y'all want to go. I started from the bottom, nigga. I grew up in a house full of mu'fuckas. That ghost-face song, 'All that I got is you', I really lived that shit, nigga! Cousins and aunts was everywhere. Nigga, I shared the same spoon and left over milk watching Saturday morning cartoons. Roaches everywhere, nigga! I really lived dat shit! Dat shit was real for me. But I knew I wanted more. I wasn't gonna let my peoples suffer like dat. I was tired of free lunch holdin' me down like steel. I had to do somethin' about it, but I ain't know what."

"Then my Uncle Bear took custody of me 'cause my mom was smokin' dat glass dick. He taught Mike and me everything he knew, and we just took it to another level. Look, I'm not goin' to get all into that because that's my story. Y'all niggaz gotta make ya own story.

This game ain't fair, nigga… ain't no love. All y'all got is y'all. Can't y'all tell? Y'all niggaz still sittin' on the step pumpin' dimes, while y'all's so-called boys losing stacks up Atlantic City. Them niggaz throwing away thousands and y'all struggling with hundreds. But I'm about to change all that. When I hit you niggaz, y'all need to go hard 0- hard as a mu'fucka! Y'all niggas gotta be cold as a December morning. If y'all gotta muscle some nigga, muscle 'em. If y'all gotta shoot a couple of mu'fuckas, shoot 'em. If y'all gotta kill a couple of mu'fuckas, kill 'em. That's how y'all gotta play… just don't bite the hand that feeds you," he warned them as he pulled up on their block to let them out.

"Look," he said as they got out the car. "Be on point, 'cause when I call, that shit is gonna be on its way," he finished, and drove away leaving them in awe.

Those young niggas were ready!

■■■■■

Tommy called Mike and told him to meet him over Kelly's house on Bennett Street at 7 o'clock. When he pulled up, Mike was already there. Tommy rang the doorbell and within a few seconds Kelly was opening the door.

"Hey, baby!" she said gingerly and greeted him with a huge hug. "Whass good?" she asked, squeezing him tightly into her breast and kissing him softly on the cheek.

"Whass'up, baby? Whass good wit 'chu?" he asked.

"Nothin. In here cookin' dinner. I figured that since you was comin' over I might as well cook somethin', you know? Y'all probably ain't ate nothin' all day," she said, letting him go so he could come inside. They hadn't eaten all day long and it was already getting dark outside.

"Where's Mike?"

"In there watching T.V.," she replied, and led Tommy into the house.

Tommy stepped into the house behind Kelly and still couldn't get over her body. Her ass had even gotten "phatter" since she came from re-hab almost eight years ago. And now as he watched it bounce loosely and freely in the summer dress she was wearing, he was glad they didn't give up on her. He and Mike had sent Kelly away to three re-habs before she finally got it together at the last one, eight years ago. Since then she had become an interior designer and they opened up a little business for her that was doing rather well.

She designed both Tommy and Mike's houses, but her shit was laid. It had a feel that instantly welcomed you in like it had arms or something. It made you feel right at home. The colors of the house and the artwork there were soothing to the mind and relaxing to the soul. Everything else was just comfortable. The incense were burning, and the bookshelves were full of African literature and urban novels of street life. The smell coming from the kitchen made your stomach growl.

"Damn! What 'chu cookin'?" Tommy asked.

"Ox tails, rice, gravy, macaroni and cheese and cabbage. I got some cake and cornbread in there too," she answered modestly.

"Is it almost done?"

"Yeah. It'll be done in a little while," she answered, and walked out to the kitchen to check on the meal.

Tommy walked out into the living room where Mike was reclined in the lazy boy watching Sports Center and flopped down on the couch. They were showing some highlights of LeBron James that was almost unreal. He actually owned the basketball court. Even Michael Jordan wasn't as dominant as he was at his age. It was almost scary to think of his future. Would he surpass MJ? Niggas all want to know.

"Whass'up, nigga?" Tommy rubbed the top of Mike's head.

"Aww man, you know me. I'm loungin' as usual. Did they say they wanted to do that?"

"Yeah, they wanna do it, but I'ma start them off light... give 'em a brick of coke and dope apiece."

"Ai'ight, that's good. I was thinking the same thing. Ain't no need to hit 'em real heavy and they ain't even got that much clientele yet, you know?"

"I feel that. But yo, other than that, what you try'na do before the summer is over? I'm thinking about flying over to London or France with my wife. Eat lunch over that mu'fucka;

153

take some pictures under the Eiffel Tower -- on some romantic shit. You know how Vita love that romantic shit."

'"What woman don't, nigga? Just let me know when. I might join you. I need to take Ann somewhere. I haven't taken her anywhere since we went to Jamaica last year," he finished as Kelly came out carrying two plates.

Kelly was Tommy and Mike's baby. She had been their baby since the first time they tricked together, when she was getting high and they were still virgins. And she was alright with playing that role in their lives, because they shared a love for each other that no one would be able to understand. They were in a three-way love affair that ran deeper than just sex. It was genuine. Their love for one another was based on care and concern, and she had their back. She would forever be grateful to them for helping her get her life back and she'd go to any limit to show that appreciation. She knew they had wives, and they knew she had a man, but they always had time for one another. They were also business partners too. Kelly was the stash house and drop-off lady.

"Thanks, old lady!" Tommy teased, as she handed them their plates.

"*Old lady!* Please! Y'all keep me young. Shiiit, I might be old enough to be y'alls mother, but I bet it ain't a young girl out there that can touch me," she said with assurance.

"She ain't lying about that one, Tommy," Mike said with a huge smile and highly arched his eyebrows.

"Boy, go 'head!" She playfully pulled Mike's plate away from him.

"Sike! Nah, I'm just playing," Mike reached for his plate and they all started eating. When they were done, Kelly knew exactly what to do next. Tommy told her to grab the bricks from the secret compartment and wait for his call. Then him and Mike left in their separate directions.

■■■■■■

"How many do you want me to grab?" Kelly asked from her pre-paid cellphone.

"Six."

"Six?" she checked to make sure.

"Yeah, six. Three cocaine and three heroin," Tommy responded from his own pre-paid cellphone.

They used the pre-paids instead of their Nextel plan phones because the pre-paid phones were untraceable.

Kelly hung up her phone and stuck it back in her pocketbook before going down into the basement. The basement in Kelly's house was fully furnished like the rest of the house, but it was a place where she entertained her company. She didn't allow anyone access to the living room. That room was for show. But the basement was where it went down. She had a 60" flat screen T.V., a pool table, a poker card table where she held her pitty-pat and tonk card games once a month. Her cherry-oak wet bar with a granite counter seated four and sat beneath a 20" mounted flat screen television. and her leather furniture seated the rest.

She walked over to the light switch on the wall and pulled off its cover. Then she stuck her hand into its opening and felt for the button. Kelly pushed the button and watched as her floor opened up. The two hydraulic arms opened a space up in the floor the size of a small vault. Inside the vault were the 560 bricks of heroin and cocaine that Tommy and Mike took from Hollywood and their cocaine connect, Flocko.

Kelly reached down into the secret compartment they had built into her floor and grabbed the 6 kilos. It wasn't hard for her to know the difference between the two, because they were wrapped differently. The cocaine was wrapped in tape and wax paper, while the heroin was wrapped in foil and wax paper. She put the six kilos into her large Coach bag, tossed it over her shoulder, and then went back to the switch. She pressed the button, put the cover back on, and watched as her floor closed back up. She walked over to where her floor just rose up and smoothed the carpet out with her foot. A person would never be able to tell that anything was ever there.

Kelly left the basement, walked out her front door and jumped in her Audi A6 and pulled off. It was time for the drop-off and she couldn't wait to get it done and over with. Her favorite show, "Strong Medicine" was about to come on Lifetime and she didn't want to miss it.

Chapter Twenty

Coming up

♫ *The blocks doin' numbers*
Everybody wants a piece of it... ♫
♪ *Twelve "K" a day* ♪
Just imagine how a week can get
♫ *When we get our shit* ♫
♫ *We get da price dat the Ricans get* ♫
♪ *740B.M.'s* ♪
♪ *Chrome rims, no leasin' it...* ♪

Oschino Vasquez – State Property

Zy, Boomer and Peacock were right where Tommy had told them to be when Kelly pulled up. She pulled over to the curb and parked, leaving her car running when she got out. Carrying the Coach bag on her shoulder, she walked towards them, but neither of them paid her any attention. They had their eyes glued to the block waiting for the drop-off so they could start coming up.

Kelly was pleased. It felt good to know that she could go unnoticed into a drug area like this, especially since she did what she did. Chances were, if they didn't know who she was by the way she looked, the police wouldn't know who she was either. She was dressed in a Kente cloth, wrap-around dress, with the top to match. Her hair was in dreadlocks and tied up in a Kente cloth, giving her the look of an African queen. Kelly looked like one of those too Black, too strong sistas that was caught up in her culture a little more than she was supposed to be. The truth was she'd learned to be when she was away. She just handled her business when she was supposed to.

"Zy, Boomer and Peacock?" she called out their names as she approached the three of them on the corner.

"Yeah," they answered in unison.

"How y'all brothas doing?" she greeted, and they looked at her puzzled.

"We ai'ight. But how you know us, sista?" Peacock greeted her back as she did them.

"I'm a friend of Tommy Good's and Mike's," she replied, and they instantly knew who she was. *She* was the drop-off.

"Alright, alright, whass'up? Damn, I thought you was one of them ladies who walked around the 'hood passing out condoms and H.I.V. pamphlets," Zy said, making Kelly smile.

"No, brotha, I'm not one of those people. I'm not a Jehovah's Witness or a Christian Crusader. I am one who understands self and the power of the One. And although I may look all pro-Black, I'm not one to judge or stereotype individuals. I'm down for mines and about my business. I'm prompt and on time. If you call, I expect you to be where you said you'd be, because I'll be there. This is not a game and I'm not trying to lecture y'all, but one slip, one miscommunication, and we all go to jail for probably a life sentence. This is the big boy league. If you ain't ready to step ya muthafuckin' game up, back the fuck down because Tommy Good and Mike will put you three lil' niggas to rest! So look, here's my number, here's the stuff and y'all call me when you got the money," she finished, and walked off carrying her empty Coach bag. She didn't even give them a chance to respond.

"Damn! She was a pretty sassy ass mutha'fucka, wasn't she?" Zy admired her beauty as he put the bricks in the bookbag he was carrying, and watched the lady who didn't even appear to be involved in the game, waltz away.

"Yeah, she is. She reminded me of the lady that played the mom on Brandy's T.V. show, 'Moesha'," Peacock said as they headed to Mom Val's house on Carter Street.

Zy sat the bookbag down on Mom Val's dining room table and pulled out the bricks. Boomer and Peacock pulled up two chairs that were around the table and scooted them next to Zy to get a better look at the coke and heroin. Boomer pulled out his house keys and dug into the corner of the brick of heroin and opened it up. The three of them looked at the brown block and frowned up their faces in a puzzled look. They had no idea that heroin was brown like this. It was so brown that it almost looked chocolate. They remembered when Tommy said he had some raw dope but that was an understatement. This shit was almost pure. He also told them that the dope could stand a seven cut, but he preferred they put a five on it. That way they'd do more than triple their money and they wouldn't be killing fiends with the poison. Because lately, niggas were dropping dead from the "fire".

Next, Peacock pulled out his keys and dug into the brick of coke that sat before him. As soon as the cocaine was exposed to the air the fumes rose up off the brick. Its scent was similar to the smell of Elmer's glue and gasoline mixed. They knew what it was instantly. They had some raw cocaine. It was like some 1988 powder -- the powder that had become nonexistent over the years due to the stretching people was doing to it. As they looked at the brick they saw the glitter on it and knew where the term "fish scale" came from. The brick actually looked like the scales on a fish. That's how raw it was. Tommy had done exactly what he said. He had put them in position and it was only a matter of time before they blew.

"Nigga, we about to get paid like the boahs, Tommy Good and Mike, nigga!" Boomer screamed overly excited.

"Yeah! And after that, niggaz gonna wanna get paid like the boahs, Peacock, Boomer and Zy, nigga!" Peacock assured them, and meant it from the bottom of his heart. He heard Tommy loud and clear when he said: *"Nigga, that"s my story. Y'all gotta make y'all's own."* And that's exactly what Peacock planned to do.

The cocaine was the only thing they knew how to fuck with like that, so they began busting it down. Peacock got up from the table and took a brick with him into the kitchen. He looked up into the cabinets and grabbed the large glass Pyrex pot and laid the brick down on the counter beside the stove. He grabbed the box of baking soda, put a little water in the pot. Then, he mixed the coke and baking soda into the water. He turned the fire on low and chefed up the cocaine on the pot until it turned into oil. When he was sure that the coke was done, he emptied three ice trays into the pot and watched as the oil turned into a huge rock on the bottom of the pot.

Meanwhile, Boomer and Zy were at the table weighing out ounces from the two bricks they still had out on the table and bagging them up in, sandwich bags. When they were finished they had 72 ounces. Boomer pulled out the calculator and did the math, coming up with a total of $57,600 at $800 apiece for an ounce. Off of the three bricks they got from Tommy and Mike, for $14,500 apiece, they would be making a profit of $14,100 off just the two. And that didn't count the brick that Peacock had out in the kitchen. So in total, off the three bricks they would make a profit of $42,900, which broke down into $14,300 apiece. That was more than enough to put them where they needed to be.

As far as the dope, they'd have to wait until tomorrow to get started on that. They still needed cut, bags and stamps. As far as the movement of the dope, they were going to do that different than the coke. They were going to sell it by the gram or the bundle. The grams would go for $60 and so would the wholes. A smart person would buy the gram. You could make almost 2-1/2 bundles. But that would be unlikely. People were so anxious and in a rush to get the quick fix and blinded by the reality that they were getting thirteen bags for $60, that they didn't even see the benefit in buying a gram. How stupid was that? Just goes to show how powerful the disease of addiction is, it'll even make you cheat yourself. That's what fiends were doing - cheating themselves.

Zy put the dope in the bookbag with the bricks of cocaine that were now broken down into ounces and zipped it up. They each kept 10 ounces apiece, five in powder and five in cooked rock; and went their separate ways.

Zy went up on the Hilltop. Boomer sat on 23rd and Carter Streets and Peacock just rode around the city broadcasting the prices he had to let everybody know they were the new bosses in town.

They were coming up!

Chapter Twenty-One

Clearing My Conscious

Watching the sun set behind a city building was a beautiful sight to see. The sky would turn a reddish, almost orange color with a purplish streak of violet or blue color from the clear sky earlier today. To Mike it went unnoticed. Hardly anything of beauty was beautiful to him anymore. Beauty had been snatched away from him nearly 17 years ago, when he discovered his twin sister's nude body in- the schoolyard Dumpster.

That picture remained fresh in his mind. No matter how he tried to erase it from his memory, it would always pop back up. He would remember him and his sister playing back home on the streets of Decatur, Georgia. He would remember the ride they took in the huge U-Haul truck to move to their new home in Delaware. He would remember her smile and the way she looked. He'd sometimes hear her voice, remember her smell, and then all of a sudden he'd feel empty. Empty because a part of him was missing.

That was the difference between having a twin, than a regular brother or sister. It was something that mourning wouldn't take away. Twins grew in the same womb together from the very beginning of their existence. They always had one another. And even though they were two separate individuals, they still functioned as one. If one got hurt, sometimes the other one would feel it. If something were to go wrong with one of them it usually would happen to the other - like catching a cold or something. So, it was more than obvious that when Michele was taken away by some maniac, that it would scar Mike until he revenged her death.

■■■■■■

Mike was driving through the city in his Spyker C8 Double 12S and decided to drive through the old neighborhood before heading home to Ann. He turned on Lombard Street and headed up past 9th and 8th Street until he came up on 7th Street to the park behind the Compton Apartments. This was the same park they used to play in as kids and seeing the kids out there playing now put a smile of Mike's face as he rode past.

He drove down to 8th Street and made a right onto Walnut Street to circle around the block. He parked beneath a tree on 7th Street and watched as they played, recapturing some of his days of happiness. He watched them run, jump, skip, climb the junglegym and wrestle in the grass. He watched the girls jump double-dutch and play patty-cake, while others played in each other's hair. But the thing that made him really gleeful was when he saw that the kids still played boys chase the girls. The feeling that Mike was having at this very moment couldn't be duplicated by any drug the doctor could prescribe, or any support groups that he could attend. The feeling he was feeling was natural and it reminded him that life wasn't always as bad as it seemed to be.

The longer Mike sat there reminiscing and watching the kids play, the darker the sky had become. He was caught up in the moment so much that he hadn't noticed that the streetlights had come on and the kids were starting to head home -- all except for a few lingered around still playing. He was just about to turn his car back on and head home himself until he noticed something in the shadows of the darkness. He squinted his eyes, looking closer, trying to get a better look at the mass object in the shadow. Then it became a perfect picture to him. It was a man dressed in dark colors stalking the kids as they played.

He decided to stay... Mike wasn't going anywhere.

■■■■■■

Deacon Matthew Johnson sat in the dark patiently awaiting his next victim. He hadn't killed in years, not since the last murder almost 17 years ago. Since then prayer must have helped him remove the evils inside of him. Help him get over the demons that he struggled to fight every day in his mind, but tonight they had come back. They had come to him just hours ago as he sat reading the Bible. The thought of how that little girl, Michele had squirmed against his power gave him an erection. The deacon was still a very sick man and he knew that only God could help him. He stood from his chair, dropped to his knees and began to pray again. The tears from his eyes were burn-blazing his cheeks and he knew why; God was punishing him for what he had done to all those little girls so many years ago. He was only getting an example of what hellfire would feel like. He stood to his feet and ran into the kitchen to splash some cold water on his face, but it didn't take away the burn. He felt the pastor tearing away at his manhood, but no one would listen. He was the kid who was trying to tear down the congregation but the people agreed with the pastor. It was the devil inside making him do it. He needed to be saved, so they baptized him. Still no one listened, so he held it inside. He had to walk around with that secret forever. He had no idea though, that the results would turn him into a monster.

He had to get out of the house.

Now here he stood in the shadows of the night... waiting. The demons won again.

The little girl ran as fast as she could around the corner in search of a hiding spot. She had no idea that there was a predator lurking in the night waiting for an opportunity to pounce an underdeveloped body. She rounded the corner at top speed, never looking back as she ran down the side of the school building. She was going to her favorite hiding spot, the one behind the dumpster. She slid behind the dumpster next to the wall and heard the boy who was chasing her run right past. She didn't move though, because he might turn around and come back this way, she thought. So she stayed right there until she thought the coast was clear.

Deacon Johnson stepped quickly from beyond the darkness and made his move. He had a clear view of the side of the school and saw exactly where the little girl went. He looked back over his shoulder to make sure the coast was clear. When he saw that it was, he became high with emotion at just the thought of what was about to happen. He approached the dumpster as quickly as he could, went behind it and the wall. And there she was scared, just how he used to be when the pastor done those horrible things to him.

Mike's heart pounded with rage. He couldn't believe what he was seeing. *Nah,* he thought. *Maybe it's just my imagination...my own paranoia.* But when he saw the man make a move after the little girl, he knew something wasn't right. He snatched his .40 caliber handgun from the glove compartment, jumped out of the car and ran after the man. He lost sight of him when he turned the corner, but something kept pulling him towards the dumpster -- the same dumpster where he found his sister. The closer he got to the dumpster, the harder his heart pounded. He could actually feel each beat in his entire body, in his ears, his chest, his neck, and his wrists... everywhere. He felt the same way he felt the day he and Tommy walked behind the dumpster together, and it made him freeze dead in his tracks. His feet became cemented to the ground.

The memories of his sister's naked body was what done it. He was afraid to see what was behind it now, but he had to. He forced himself to take another step and before he knew it, he was inched up to the dumpster. The sound of a struggle was what motivated him more. He had to save the little girl. It was the only way to avenge his sister's death and clear his conscious of the memory that haunted him every day.

He pulled the gun from the small of his back and eased down the side of the wall behind the dumpster. What he saw sent the vibe of murder through his body.

"NIGGA, WHAT DA FUCK...!"

■■■■■■

She tried to scream, but his massive hand was covering her mouth and nose. She tried to kick and scratch, but it did nothing to him. He was too big and strong for her. She fought and fought with every inch of survival that she had in her body, and was giving the man some problems until he tired her out. She put up too much of a struggle in the beginning out of fear and wasted her energy, so she began to cry.

Deacon Johnson took his hand from her nose so she could breathe, because he didn't want to kill her yet. The sobs that his hand forced back now escaped through her nostrils and the sound made his erection stiffer. "God, please forgive me for what I'm about to do!" he prayed in a whisper, only scaring the little girl more than she already was. When she heard him start praying she knew she was about to die.

Deacon Johnson began tearing away at her clothes piece by piece until she laid there naked, innocent -- not one hair on her body. He used his free hand to pull his erection from his pants and was about to do the inhumane when he heard:

"NIGGA, WHAT THE FUCK YOU DOIN'!" and he felt a kick to his ass from the back. A long painful moan escaped his mouth as he rolled over off the young innocent little girl, and she screamed at the top of her lungs to the high heavens.

"Com'ere, baby," Mike said, and she ran to the man holding the gun on her attacker. She clung to Mike's wrist so tightly that it almost hurt him. "Are you okay, baby?" he asked.

"Here... put this on," he stated, taking his T-shirt off and giving it to her so she could cover up her nude body.

"Yes," she faintly nodded, quaking with fear.

"Where do you live?"

"Around there," she managed to say between sobs, and pointed in the direction of her house.

"Okay, here's what I need for you to do. I need you to run home, tell your mommy what just happened to you. Then, tell her to call the police. When they get to your house, you bring them around here, okay? Can you do that?" He needed her to understand him. She nodded her head "yes". "Okay, good. Now go ahead," he said, and she took off running.

Mike stared at the face of the man lying on his back and couldn't believe his eyes. It was the Deacon from the neighborhood church.

"You no-good mutha'fucka! I'ma blow you got-damn brains out!" he promised. "You been frontin' in this community like you a true man of God, perpetratin' and fraudin' everybody.

"No, Michael! Wait! Your mother raised you better than that. I'ma sick man, Michael. I've been sick since I was child. No one would listen to me. I didn't mean to do what I did to your sister!" he confessed, because he felt as though he was apologizing to Michele through Michael. She and Mike were fraternal twins, and as the deacon looked into Michael's face, he saw visions of Michele's face instead of Mike's. He thought for a minute it was actually her that he was talking to.

"What did you say, mutha'fucka? You said you *'sorry about my sister*?'" he asked in grief, flashing back to the day they found Michele.

"I didn't mean to hur—" he tried to say, but he never got a chance to finish because Mike blanked out. He raised his foot and began stomping the life out of Deacon Johnson. The first stomp knocked all the teeth out of his mouth and gushed blood all over his wheat-colored, nubuck Timberlands, but he continued to stomp his face.

When he finished, the deacon was dead. He had crushed his entire skull and facial structure into jelly. The sight was sickening. Mike had literally stomped the bones out of the deacon's face causing them to protrude from his skin. His right eyeball hung from its socket and his nose was completely missing from his face, but that wasn't enough for Mike. He bent down and began stripping the deacon until he was naked, and then emptied his clip into the dead man's chest. After that, Mike reached down and tore the eyeball away from the meat it was connected to and put it in his front pocket. Then he picked the deacon's lifeless body up and threw it in the dumpster.

When he slammed the door shut on the dumpster, he shut the door in his mind closed -- the one that plagued him for years. He looked up to the sky and stared at the brightest star he could find and said, "I told you I was going to get him, baby sis!" and smiled as he looked toward the sky walking to his car.

Mike's conscious was clear.

Chapter Twenty-Two

At Night I Can't Sleep... I Toss & Turn

Tommy and Mike were headed down 1-95 towards the city of Baltimore when the snow began to fall. It wasn't sticking to the ground much but what little that did, managed to paint the grass alongside of road white. Reports that the storm would worsen wasn't enough to make them change their minds about their mission. They were about to do the unthinkable go with Plan B... rob Hollywood.

Tommy sat in the passenger seat as Mike drove up to the tollbooth. He tossed the change into the basket and resumed the speed limit approaching the Baltimore Tunnel. Tommy was silent, deep in thought. He felt uncertain about what was about to go down. Not because of fear or anything like that, but because of his woman. He was thinking about what it would do to her. Davita loved her brother to death. And even though she knew his life would end up in jail or violently murdered in the streets, she would never believe the love of her life would have a hand in his death.

"Fuck it!" Mike told him as they contemplated the move. "She know the nigga gonna die like dat anyway," he predicted and Tommy agreed. Those were his exact same thoughts anyway; he just needed to hear them confirmed by Mike so he wouldn't feel so bad about betraying his wife.

Normally, Hollywood wouldn't have allowed anyone to get that close to him other than those already in his camp, but he made a costly mistake. He allowed his personal relationship between him and Tommy to interfere with business. He had taken a personal liking to Tommy the first time he met him. He couldn't do anything but respect him or Mike for being able to come up by themselves. Anyone that could muscle their way through the streets and become rich enough for people to start acknowledging them from state to state had to be respected.

It didn't hurt that he was his sister's future husband and father of their baby she was carrying. That just made it all the more reason for Hollywood to take him in as a little brother. He taught Tommy about the heroin game and advised him on every move he made with the drug. The results: Tommy and Mike tripled their money in only a year's time. Hollywood embraced them like family selling them kilos of heroin weekly, for the same price he got it for but they were unaware of that. Only if Mike and Tommy knew the sincere love he had for them. Hollywood had no idea that his refusal to personally introduce Tommy and Mike to the connect -- the Mexican cartel -- would be his demise.

Truth was, Hollywood feared that once he introduced them to the connect knowing that they were purchasing more heroin then he was, the connect would give them better numbers. And because Tommy and Mike were moving so many kilos of heroin throughout Philly, New Jersey, New York, Boston and Connecticut, it would only be a matter of time before they conquered D.C.

"I'm tellin' you man," Tommy pleaded to Hollywood, "Turn me and Mike onto the connect. That way youll still have your connects down here and in the South and me and Mike could handle the North. This way we won't have to wait until you're ready to score again. It's fuckin' up our business!"

But Hollywood had shot them down. He was greedy and his greed would cost him his life. Tommy watched the same thing happen to his Philly boys, Sha-Rock and Killer Cal, but Skip was the smart one. They'd never catch him slippin'. In fact, that's why they were headed to the Murphy Homes Projects now, because Skip was already in Baltimore. He had called them earlier in the evening and informed them that he had kidnapped the boy, Lil'

Shawn from the picture they gave him and was waiting for them at a motel off of the Beltway.

Skip never ceased to amaze them. He was their secret weapon and he moved like a ghost. They never saw him anywhere until it was time to meet somewhere to do work; and it's been that way from the day they met him. They never knew what type of car he was in, and didn't know where he lived. All they knew was that he was Uncle Bear's boy, and they remembered him, Sha-Rock and Killer Cal from back in the day when they were young boys. They learned a lot from Skip just by watching the way he moved, and by doing that they also learned why Uncle Bear was so secretive.

That's where Hollywood fucked up at. He let a cold-blooded snake into his house and made it his friend. He let down his guard and revealed too much of his business to Tommy. Hollywood should have listened to that old story his boy's pop had told them about the man and the snake. He said:

"A man took in a poisonous wounded snake in his home and doctored it back to health. Once the snake got completely healthy it bit the man. The man looked at the snake in shock as poison shot through his body, and right before he died he asked the snake, 'Why did you bite me?' The snake replied, 'I'm a snake, what did you expect? I'm slimy!'"

Now Hollywood was about to get bitten by his very own snake.

Mike pulled into the motel's parking lot and parked, while Tommy dialed Skip's number. Before the phone could even ring two full times, they were caught off-guard by a knock on the window.

"Oh shit!" Tommy jumped as he pulled out his .45 handgun.

"Hello!" Skip said into his phone, smiling in front of them as he held it up to his ear.

"Damn, nigga! You's a bad mu'fucka! We ain't even see you comin'. Where were you?" Tommy asked, startled.

"I'm everywhere, nigga," Skip taunted them.

"I'm sure glad you was my Uncle Bear's people and y'all raised us up from pups, 'cause I'd hate to be on the other side," Tommy said as he and Mike exited the car.

"What did I tell y'all? Didn't I say always check your surroundings? If I wasn't true to my word, and if Bear wasn't my mutha'fuckin' brother from another mother, I woulda been put the pistol to one of y'alls head and made you repeat after me. So come on y'all, let's say it together... This is for Sha-Rock, Killer Cal and Bear."

And they said it together: *"You caught me slippin'."*

Then they walked into the motel room.

The room was the last one on the backside of the building. There weren't any occupants next to them because the curtains to the room were open. That was a good thing, but dreadful for their guest. They were far away from the front office to do what they had to do and no one would hear them. Skip opened the door and there was Lil' Shawn, Hollywood's hit man.

"Look at dis shit!" Tommy said when he entered the room, "I know yo' bitch-ass wasn't in here cryin'! Not hard-ass Lil' Shawn! I knew your punk-ass was a bitch the first time I saw you!" He glared at Lil' Shawn who was tied up in a chair with duct tape on his mouth.

"The nigga was trying to play hard at first," Skip told them. "But I eventually broke his punk-ass down," he said and flexed his muscles. Skip was a big motherfucker. That bid that he did up in Jersey had blew his ass up like "The Hulk". Them Oodles of Noodles and bread could make the littlest man big.

"Well, I'ma break this nigga down a little more, you heard me?" Mike said, and smiled *that* smile. Mike had the exact same smile as the fat soldier who was sitting on the toilet in the movie "Full Metal Jacket" after the sergeant had broken him. And Tommy knew by the look -- Mike had switched over to his "maniac stage".

"Now *do* you see that face, nigga? Look into those eyes," Tommy ridiculed. "Now that's a mu'fuckin' killer!" and Lil' Shawn began to cry again like a bitch. He saw the death in Mike's eyes.

Mike walked straight up to him as he sat helplessly in the chair and smacked the shit out of him.

"Tommy, go get the pliers outta da car," Mike mandated, never taking his eyes off of Lil' Shawn, and Tommy was back within a few minutes. He handed Mike the pliers and had no idea what Mike was going to do. Skip had already informed them that Lil' Shawn gave up the information needed, but Mike didn't think so. He thought Lil' Shawn was still holding some shit back.

"Nigga, I'ma ask you one mutha'fuckin' time, you hear me? Now, what else is it that we need to know? And you better say somethin'."

Lil' Shawn didn't answer. He really had already told Skip everything.

"Nigga, you gotta snatch the tape offa his mouth!" Tommy laughed.

"Oh shit! Yeah, dat's right... dat's why da nigga ain't sayin' shit!'" Mike responded, still able to find some humor in the madness. "Nigga, say sumpt'n!" Mike ordered, snatching the tape from his mouth. But Lil' Shawn still didn't say anything.

Maybe he don't know anything else, Mike thought, but he still wanted to have some fun. That's when he went to work. He jammed the pliers into Lil' Shawn's mouth, gripped them onto his teeth and with a quick precise twist of the wrist, *"Pop!"* broke them mu'fuckas right off.

Tommy and Skip turned their heads.

"Damn, nigga! You crazy as hell!" Skip said, rubbing his tongue against his front teeth at the thought of what Mike just did. He only knew of one other mutha'fucka as crazy as him, and that was his mans, Killer Cal, God bless his soul.

■■■■■■

"Get off of me!" young Sinque yelled at the top of his lungs. His scream coincided with those from Lil' Shawn as Mike ripped out his teeth.

"Shut up! It's mine!" Xavier, Tommy's other son, snapped the toy back from him.

"It is not! *Stop!*"

"Is too!" Xavier said, tossing Sinque to the floor.

"I'ma tell daddy! *Da-a-a-d-e-e-!* Xavier messin' wit' me!" Sinque hollered and burst through the bedroom door.

Tommy jumped straight up in the bed and placed his head into his hands. He then ran his fingers over his hair and tried to shake the memory from his head, but the dream was a reality. It was as clear in his head to him as the day it happened. He heard Lil' Shawn's teeth snap off. He heard the smack and the screams. What Mike did to him that night would stain his memory forever. It was one of the crudest things you could imagine. The torture was so bad that Lil' Shawn begged for Mike to kill him, but he refused. He just kept applying pain. It was horrible -- so horrible that Tommy and Skip had to leave the room.

Tommy looked at his two sons standing at the foot of his bed and said, "What I tell y'all about dat shit? If y'all can't play together, don't play at all, And Sinque, why you always crying?"

"'Cause he messin' wit' me!" he whined.

"Xavier, why you keep fuckin' wit' him?"

"I ain't messin' wit' him, Dad. He a punk! He got my GameBoy," Xavier, the younger one said.

"You got his GameBoy?"

"No."

"Do too!"

"Do not!"

"Man, shut up wit' dat whining bullshit! Where da mu'fuckin' GameBoy? Here, gimme dat shit! Ain't nobody playin' wit' dat shit now! Y'all get on my nerves wit' dis bullshit! Where y'all mom?" Tommy asked his sons.

"Her and Danita went to the store to get some cereal. She said they'll be right back," Sinque answered.

Danita was their firstborn. Tommy and Davita had her a year after they got back together, and a year before Hollywood's death. That was in 1999, right before the new millennium kicked in.

Hollywood was robbed and brutally murdered. The news of his death was headlined for weeks, and Davita despised it. She hated the way they talked about her brother. They painted him out to be the worst menace to society of all time; and even had the nerve to say in so many words that they were happy. One headline read:

"At Least the Streets of D.C. Are Safe To Walk Again".

Tommy got out of bed and walked into the bathroom connected to the master bedroom to brush his teeth. When he spit the toothpaste out of his mouth into the bowl it splattered on Davita's side.

"Shit! Now I gotta hear her mouth." Tommy had done it again. He had used her sink instead of his and she hated the way he left toothpaste in her sink. That's why when they bought this house last year. She made sure it had his and hers vanity sets in the bathroom. "Fuck it! A sink is a sink," he told himself, and finished brushing his teeth and washing his face.

He looked over on the little stand and grabbed the *Jet* magazine and decided to take a seat on the toilet. No sooner had the article gotten good about a homeless woman, the door opened up.

"Oh my God, baby! Wait 'til you see this!" Davita said, busting into the bathroom while he was trying to take a private shit.

"Damn, man! Shut da door! Don't you know how to knock? A nigga can't even take a shit in peace!" he complained.

It seemed like *every* time he had to use the bathroom, she'd bust right in. It didn't bother her one bit if she wanted to talk. She would sit on the edge of the tub or stand in the doorway, but not this morning; Tommy wanted to shit in peace.

"Get out! Not this morning, damn! Can I shit in peace today?" he said, trying to hold the door shut.

"Yeah, baby, but this is for real. Look!" she said, handing him the newspaper. "They found Deacon Johnson dead!"

Tommy grabbed the newspaper through the cracked door and quickly shut it back. Davita mumbled something under breath, but he didnt hear her. His response was, "I don't need you in here to read the paper!"

Tommy looked at the front page of the newspaper and saw the photo of Deacon Johnson. Under it the storyline read:

"Little Girl Attacked by Deacon - Deacon Later Found Dead".

He was more shocked than anything as he began to read the article word for word, skipping not a single detail. When he turned to the inside page and saw the photo of the dumpster where the deacon's body was found it sent a chill up his spine. The dumpster was in the same location as the dumpster that he and Mike found Michele's body in.

The more Tommy read along, the more sense it began to make to him. *The little girl's statement of what happened sounded like the same exact thing that happened to Michele,* he thought. The police stated in the article that they were looking for the man who saved her, to question him on the accounts of what took place. They also said that he wasn't a suspect and no charges would be filed against him.

My ass if they ain't! As soon as he says, "I'm the one who saved the girl's life", he's going to jail, Tommy told himself as he finished up the article.

The way they discovered the deacon's body was gruesome. The reports said that when they found him, the deacon's head had been stomped completely to the point where one of his eyes had popped out. The term they used was medical, but Tommy knew that's what they meant. *Serves his ass right!* He thought about the deacon trying to rape the little girl. *They should have stomped that niggas balls off too!* Tommy thought aloud, glad for whoever done it.

When he finished reading the entire article word for word twice, he knew that the deacon was responsible for the rape and murder of Michele. He walked out of the bathroom and headed straight over to the house phone and began dialing Mike's number. He had to tell him about what he was thinking.

"Baby, ain't that crazy?" Davita asked.

"Fuck him! Dat nigga probably did that shit to Michele," Tommy said to Davita, and he gave her his theory. When he was done, she agreed that maybe it was possible.

"Hello," Mike answered…

■■■■■■

When Mike got home last night, Ann was sitting up in the living room waiting for him. The kids were already in bed sleep. His dinner plate was neatly wrapped in plastic wrap in the microwave, and she was ready to roleplay. Little did she know there wouldn't be any of that tonight. Tonight she wouldn't be able to play the "naughty little Catholic schoolgirl" who was sneaking with her thugged out boyfriend. But she still looked good though.

Ann was sitting on the couch with two braided pig-tails in her hair, a white crisp shirt, a blue/green/white plaid skirt with white stocking socks and a patent leather pair of little girl Easter shoes - the ones with the big rounded-off toes and single strap across the foot they called Mary Janes. Had she known what Mike had just witnessed, a little girl would have been the last thing she tried to imitate. She would have gone along with the "stripper" or the "nurse"... maybe even the "cheerleader". *Nah, the "police",* she thought. *Yeah, he would've liked that. Then he really would've been able to say "Fuck the police!" while he was fucking me,* she thought to herself, because that's exactly how she felt. She didn't want to make love tonight... she wanted to *fuck.* She knew Mike loved it when she felt nasty like this. She loved it too. That's what kept them so madly in love with one another all these years, because they never ran out of ways to please each other or keep their relationship fresh and new.

Mike walked in the house and Ann's plans of a beautiful night were replaced by horror. From his chest down to his boots, he was covered in blood. Some of it had dried up, but for the most part it was still wet. He kicked off his bloody boots at the door, but even his socks were bloody around the tops of them.

"What happened?" she asked her man like a concerned woman would do instead of becoming hysterical and going crazy and shit. She knew from experience that getting all hysterical only made matters worse, so she played it cool.

"I had to handle some business," he said with a smile, but it wasn't that crazy looking smile. It was bright smile -- a happy smile -- one she hadn't seen since the kids were born, so she knew it had to be something good. But why was he so bloody? She decided not to ask. She'd wait for him to tell her probably later on that night when they were cuddled in bed. Besides, since he wasn't worried about the blood, neither was she. This wasn't the first time she saw him all bloody like this and it probably wouldn't be the last time. She knew what type of lifestyle he lived and she had heard all the stories about him and Tommy. But none of that mattered to her.

"Aren't you scared of him?" some of her girlfriends would ask, knowing all about Mike. But being scared of him never crossed her mind, and never had since Tommy's 12th birthday party when they were kids. In fact, she still got butterflies in her stomach when she saw him.

"I had to handle some long overdue business, baby," he repeated, breaking her chain of thought.

"What kind of business?" she decided to ask sensing his wanting to talk.

"I found out who killed Michele."

"What!" she asked surprised. "Who?"

"Deacon Johnson," he answered, and she was speechless. "That's right, baby. Deacon mu'fuckin' Johnson! I murdered dat bastard too!" he said, and reached in his pocket. "Go get the pickle jar out the refrigerator and empty it out first," he directed and pulled the deacon's eye from his pocket.

Ann couldn't believe what she was hearing, and if she wasn't crazy herself for being around Mike this long, she was when she saw that eyeball. She just went into the kitchen, emptied the pickle jar in the sink, and brought it back to him. Mike dropped it in the jar and handed it back to her. "Go put some vinegar in there to preserve it for me, and put it up 'til I get out of the shower."

"Okay," she replied, still remaining calm, but she didn't know how much longer she could. Her hands were trembling and she was a nervous wreck. She couldn't believe that in her hand she held the deacon's eye. She couldn't let Mike see her fear though.

180

She was his backbone. If she fell apart, then what would happen to him? Ann knew Michele's death had driven him crazy but she never left his side. She stuck with him through everything. She knew he wasn't crazy and Tommy knew it also. He was just traumatized over Michele's death. Now that he had gotten some closure, she knew for sure that he'd be better... at least she hoped so.

As soon as she heard the shower water cut on, she ran to the trashcan and threw up. When he got out of the shower, she was dressed in a police uniform.

"Baby, you're under arrest!" she said. "Now put your hands up!"

"Why, what did I do?"

"Carried that concealed weapon!" she responded, and snatched the towel from around his waist.

"It's only a gun, officer," he played along.

"Well that's a mighty *big* gun!"

"I need a big gun, officer. I'm going hunting."

"Hunting? Where are you hunting at?"

"In your bushes!" and they fell out laughing. They couldn't hold the straight faces any longer.

That night, after some good lovemaking, Mike slept like a baby for the first time in seventeen years.

The next morning, he was awakened by the sound of the phone ringing.

"Hello," he answered.

"Hey, baby boy. You sleep?"

"Nah, I'm wide awoke. I slept like a baby last night."

"I heard dat," Tommy replied. He wanted to tell him about the deacon and what he thought but he didn't want to jump right out and say it. He knew how delicate the situation was with Mike when it came to his sister. "Yo, did you read this morning's paper?" Tommy asked.

"Nah, not yet. Why?"

"Man, they got the deacon from the church on the front page. Said they found him in a dumpster. Somebody killed his ass. Apparently it was the Good Samaritan who saved this little girl from being raped by him," Tommy explained as his words refreshed Mike's memory.

The more he talked, the more relieved he felt. A ton of pressure had been lifted from his shoulders. That was really the only reason why he continued to dwell on his sister's death. He did it because he felt he at least owed her to avenge her death and he wouldn't rest until he got it.

He got up out of bed while Ann slept peacefully and crept out into the kitchen, while Tommy continued to read him the article over the phone. He opened the pantry door where Ann kept all the canned goods neatly stacked on the shelves, and there it was -- his souvenir -- the deacon's eyeball floating in vinegar. *I can't wait to show Tommy,* Mike thought, and smiled. Tommy had a vague idea but wasn't sure if Mike had done the deacon in, and neither did anyone else. That secret was Mike's, Ann's and the deacon's for now. No one else would ever find out, except for Tommy.

They hung up the phones.

Chapter Twenty-Three

Look Who's Getting Money Now...

Yeah, That's Us!

♪ Damn it feels good to see people ♫
Up on it,
♫ Flip two keys in two weeks
And didn't flaunt... ♫
My brain is haunted
♪ Wit' mean dreams
GS's wit' B.B.'s on it.....♪

Biggie Smalls a.k.a Notorious B.I.G.

The word was finally out... Boomer, Zy and Peacock had officially taken over the driver's seat to Tommy and Mike's program. And even though people knew it, it took nearly a month before the weight sales started picking up. Reason being, because the other niggas didn't want to expose their hands to the young boys. Not just a few weeks ago they were asking them for work. The main reason they didn't want to do work with the young boys though was because the majority of them were broke. Yeah, it's true. These same niggas riding around in the new cars with all the ice on their necks, are the same ones buying 4-1/2's. No wonder they couldn't give them any work! They were working with the same 4-1/2 ounces themselves.

They had a trick for that though. Since niggas was being stubborn and wanting to spend their money with them, they decided to corner the market. They knew it would be impossible for anyone to compete with them because they had too much coke. And the price they were getting it at, they could afford to basically do what they wanted. So they started moving rocks out of 12/12 shiny zip-lock bags like it was candy. They figured since Tommy and Mike were charging them only $400 an ounce for the cocaine, they could double the size of the rocks people were selling and cook the cocaine down to the oils. They wouldn't be selling that baked up cocaine with all the baking soda mixed in it.

When you're trying to corner the marker, that's what you have to do. You have to have the biggest shit; the best coke and not worry about doubling your money. It's not about that. It's about the fast flip. So that's what they did. They flipped fast and they managed to corner the market. The plan: take all the coke money away from the city. Make the smokers from every side of town come buy their rocks. Eventually dealers in the city would respect their handle. They would have to bow down -- willingly or unwillingly. And once they did, they already planned to give the blocks back. But as for now, the two for five rocks had Carter Street and 4th and Clayton Street jumping.

"Yo, yo, yo! Got them two for five rocks!" one of the young workers pumping for Boomer, Zy and Peacock shouted, sounding like the shit off the Wu-Tang Clan's "36 Chambers" album.

The scene was crazy to them as they sat on Aunt Val's steps and watched their block packed with people. Just last month they couldn't knock off 4-1/2 ounces in a week. Now they were knocking off almost 1-1/2 bricks a week selling nickel rocks. The best part about it though was that Tommy and Mike weren't applying any pressure. They weren't pressed for the money. They knew it was going to take some time to get their clientele in order even though they sent all their customers to them. People were just funny like that. They didn't want to deal with the middleman; they wanted to do business with the boss. Thing was, they were the bosses now.

But it didn't matter to Tommy and Mike either way. They knew that eventually if they wanted to get some raw cocaine or some raw dope at a good price, they were going to have to get it from their boys. Right now though, Tommy and Mike were just happy to see them getting money.

Boomer, Zy and Peacock had the same look on their faces and in their eyes as he and Mike had back in the day. It was the look of hunger. The look of wanting a better life than the one they were living now. One that extended way beyond the row of boarded up row homes that surrounded them. And they knew they would get there as long as they had Tommy and Mike on their side. They would be rich by next year. Then the second part of Tommy's plan would kick in.

As for now, they were just going to keep using the full coverage insurance Tommy and Mike had on them. They were like State Farm. As long as people knew, Tommy and Mike had their backs. There wasn't a single person in the city that would even entertain the thought of doing something to them. That's how much they feared Tommy and Mike. Boomer, Zy and Peacock had the keys to the city without the Mayor even giving it to them, and they took it.

"Fuck Mayor Baker! I wanted Bovell to win anyway," Boomer disrespectfully stated after Peacock said they had the key to the city and Baker hadn't given it to them.

"I wanted Bovell to win too," Zy added. "Man, dat nigga from da 'hood! He's for da people as a whole, nigga! Young people, old people, the kids! All dat! Black people, Puerto Ricans, White people, it don't matter. If you're a minority, he got your back! Word, he do. Oh, and you know what else? If dat nigga get a suggestion from the community and it's proper... I mean, to benefit the people... he goin' to take dat shit to the legislator's hall his damn self! He ain't just goin' to make a bunch of promises!" Zy finished.

"Yeah, but dat nigga also don't play when it come to this drug shit!" Boomer reminded them.

"I mean, come on cousin. What 'chu expect? Nigga, dis shit ain't legal. If I was the Mayor or running for Mayor, I'd made it hard for drug dealers too, feel me?" Peacock reasoned.

"Nah, nigga, you talkin' crazy now," Boomer snapped.

"No I ain't, nigga. You talkin' crazy. I don't like being no drug dealer, nigga. You think I like seeing my peoples all fucked up on this drug shit? Hell no! I do this shit 'cause I got to. But if I were the Mayor, nigga, niggaz like us wouldn't have to pump, 'cause I'd make sure it was some good jobs out this mu'fucka. Good paying ones at that. That's what Robert Bovell is about, nigga. He about bailing out da city. In more ways than one, too. Bailing niggaz outta jail. Bailing niggaz outta poverty. Bailing niggaz outta drug addiction and putting them in programs. Bailing niggaz outta homelessness. Bailing niggaz out period! Bailing the community out!

I know what. I ain't got no felonies, nigga. I'm voting for Bovell again. Just like everybody else in Wilmington needed to do. Old people too. Shit, if they want their kids and grandkids to be in good hands when they dead and gone, they better vote Bovell too!" Peacock ran it.

"Man, fuck dat shit right now, nigga! I need to get dis money now so I'll be able to retire by the time he is elected, feel me?" Zy said jokingly, and they all fell out laughing.

"Nigga, you crazy as a mu'fucka!" Boomer said, still laughing.

Chapter Twenty-Four

A Trip To The Past

Kelly called Tommy and Mike both to inform them that she had just dropped off another six kilos to Boomer, Zy and Peacock. Things were really picking up for them on the weight tip, and Tommy couldn't have been more pleased.

There was always a plan behind a plan behind a plan for him. And Boomer, Zy and Peacock were making it all come together. A nigga had to actually go to Miami for anywhere near the prices Tommy and Mike were giving to Boomer, Zy and Peacock. But he did it for a reason. There was a method behind his madness. He hadn't paid a penny for the drugs and he just wanted to get rid of them. He knew by letting them go cheap, that would be another quick $2.5 million added on to the other two-digit million stacks he had accumulated through the drug game and the stock market.

He also knew by doing that Boomer, Zy and Peacock would blow up quickly. That would be perfect timing because for some odd reason he felt the long arm of the law closing in on him. He knew by them blowing up so fast that that would definitely take him out of the spotlight. Tommy leaned back on the couch after hanging the phone up with Kelly and dozed off reflecting back on that night he couldn't forget....

...He couldn't stand to watch it anymore and neither could Skip. The sight of seeing Mike use those pliers was too much to stomach, even for him. He actually broke off everyone of Lil' Shawn's teeth. Then after that, he began snatching each and every one of his fingernails off with the pliers.

"Nigga is dat all?" Mike asked for the thousandth time, but Lil' Shawn hadn't stop screaming yet.

Tommy and Skip thought for sure that they would be heard, so they stepped out of the room for extra caution. There was''t a person in sight, but they still decided to stay outside anyway. Mike is going crazy! *Skip thought.* I ain't going back in that mutha'fucka!

Tommy read the expression on Skip's face and knew just what Skip was thinking. *"He ain't going crazy... he is crazy!"* Tommy told him.

Meanwhile, inside the room, Mike was pacing the floor in circles. *"Nigga, I said is that all?" he asked again, looking at Lil' Shawn in the eyes.* The deeper he stared in them, the more aggravated he became. Lil' Shawn was a bitch. He hated that shit more than anything else in the world, when a nigga played hard as nails but was really soft as a waterbed. "Smack!" *The sounds of Mike's palms connecting to the sides of Lil' Shawn's face echoed through the room, sending the already dripping blood from his mouth flying and splattering up against the wall and over the lampshade.*

"I told thoo everyding thath I know! Pleath man... don'th keep doin' thiths tho me!" he begged as the words coming from his mouth sounded funny. He couldn't get his T's or S's to come out right because he didn't have no teeth in his mouth.

"Nigga, I'm tellin' you now, if we get all the way over there and your punk-ass lying, that little bit of shit I just did do you ain't gonna be shit! That lil' ripping your fingernails off and pulling your teeth out ain't nothin' compared to what I'ma do to you. Wait 'til I smash your balls up in these mu'fuckas!" he threatened, and clamped them together tightly.

Mike wrapped a whole new piece of duct tape over his mouth and untied him from the chair. He grabbed him by the arm and led him out to The Hearse and threw him in the back seat before getting in there with him. Tommy jumped in the drive's seat and Skip hopped in the passenger seat and they drove off.

Lil' Shawn was taking them to the stash spot, and to their surprise, it wasn't the Murphy Homes Projects. The stash spot was a little apartment Hollywood rented down by the Harbor. Tommy was glad Mike was convinced that Lil' Shawn knew more. If that wouldn't have been the case, ain't no telling what would have happened if they went up in the projects. After all, they were in the "murder capitol".

When Tommy came back from his flashback, he looked down at his wrist for the time. It was almost nine o'clock. *Davita should be on her way home,* he thought, calculating the time it took her to get from D.C. back to Delaware. She left early this morning to take the kids to see her mother, plus she wanted to check on her other office.

Davita was Mrs. Davita Good, M.D., and Dr. Good for short. Her patients liked to call her Dr. Good for short, because no matter how they felt when they arrived, they always felt good when they left, as did their feet. Davita was living her dream and she had a wonderful husband who helped her make it all come true. Her dream was to become a podiatrist, but the second part was to open up a practice smack dead in the center of D.C.'s ghetto. And right after graduating at the top of her class from Johns Hopkins University, she was able to do that. A year later Tommy helped her open another office in the heart of Wilmington.

Tommy picked up his phone and called Mike to see how he was doing. He hadn't talked to him but twice this week and the last time was early yesterday morning. After their conversation, he went over Mike's house, and that's when his suspicions were answered... Mike had murdered the Deacon.

Here it was almost another whole day and he hadn't heard from him yet. This wasn't like Mike at all. It seemed as if ever since the deacon was handled, he had become a totally different person. He wasn't the same Mike who called every hour on the hour, needing Tommy to talk to him about the things that were bothering him. He was the old Mike... the one Tommy met years ago, and it was taking Tommy some time to get used to. He was just as normal now as he was before his sister was brutally murdered. And Tommy was completely happy for his boy, but he knew that deep down inside that other side of him still existed... especially after he showed Tommy that eyeball floating around in the jar of vinegar.

"Whass'up, nigga? Damn, what... 'chu forgot a nigga's number?" Tommy asked as Mike answered the phone.

"Nah, nigga, whass good? You know I ain't forgot your number, nigga," Mike responded.

"Well whass'up? Whass good? What 'chu doin'?"

"I ain't doin' shit... sittin' here looking at the sheriff's sales in the paper. I'm looking for apartments or houses in foreclosure. I'm thinking about buying an apartment complex. Ann said she thinks it's a good idea. You gotta start doin' something with that stock market money, nigga. We ain't try'na go broke before we can make some serious investments on some legal shit. Feel me?"

"Nigga, I ain't worrying about going broke; we got plenty of change."

"I ain't mean it like dat, nigga. I meant it jokingly. But we still need to invest while we got proof of where all our money is coming from."

"I feel dat. What you think Marcus is doing? You know he still fuckin' wit' stocks. Anyway, whass'up? Did you think about that vacation I asked you about?"

"Yeah, damn right I've been thinking about that! Where you wanna go?"

"First I wanna take the kids down Disney World, and then after that I'm try'na take a life changing experience trip to Africa with Vita."

"Africa?" Mike asked puzzled.

"Yeah, nigga... Africa. I'll be damn if I wanna keep going to Cancun, Jamaica, the Bahamas and all them places. Fuck dat shit. I want to go to the 'Motherland', nigga! Feel me? Africa is the most beautiful place on this planet, nigga. And it's fucked up that we got a nerve to be Black and been everywhere but there. That's our problem now. We all go support these Island mu'fuckas but won't support our own. And when I say 'Island people', I'm not talking about the Jamaicans or the Trinidadian people, 'cause they our people too. I'm talking about them Mexicans and shit, feel me?"

"I feel you," Mike answered as he listened to Tommy more attentively than when he first started off.

"See, the T.V. and shit, like the news, be having a nigga think that Africa just consists of people in the bushes and shit. Nigga, that ain't Africa. Africa is beautiful. They won't show us that part though. They show us the bullshit. They afraid if they show a nigga them huge-ass buildings made of gold and the beautiful cities of West Africa's Ivory Coast, or cities like Johannesburg, that a nigga might want to start migrating back, feel me? That's why all they show is all the poverty shit. I bet if I go up Philly or downtown Wilmington and take some footage wit' my camcorder and show mu'fuckas over there them bums and winos that be sleeping on cardboard boxes and shit, I bet they wouldn't want to come over here either, now would they?" Tommy said, making more sense than just some science.

"Hell no! Damn, cousin, I never looked at it like that. You just made me see some shit I never would have looked at. Nigga, it ain't a place in the world that could make me change my mind now! We goin' to Africa!" Mike insisted.

"Ai'ight, Africa it is. Let me call Lil' Marcus and get him to handle the reservations. Oh, by the way... did he tell you our shares are up two points from when we brought them?"

"Which ones?"

"Microsoft!" he said full of energy. "Bill Gates is da man!"

"I shoulda known," Mike said. "Baby!" he called out to Ann.

"Huh?" she asked, stepping around the corner dressed like a cheerleader, except Ann was topless and holding pom-poms.

"We're going to Africa," he said without looking up.

"Africa?" she asked confused, with the same puzzled look on her face that he first had.

"Yeah, Africa!" he replied.

"Okay," she said. "But right now you just scored a touchdown!"

And Mike looked up from his paper. Instantly he became hard as a brick. *Damn, I love this girl!* he thought.

Chapter Twenty-Five

Africa

Tommy and Mike hadn't the slightest idea why Marcus would book the two vacations back to back. They heard of getting it done and over with, but damn! They barely had enough time to get the kids to their babysitters before the next flight took off from the Philadelphia International Airport. Its destination: the Ivory Coast of West Africa.

This was the vacation trip that they were looking forward to. The one with the children in Orlando, Florida at Disney World was fun for them too, but it was for the kids. That didn't matter though, because Tommy, Mike, Davita and Ann still enjoyed themselves. They had just as much fun, if not more, than the children did. Disney World just had that affect on people. It really was a magical experience for everybody from ages 8-80. It just made you feel like a kid again.

Dressed in Mickey Mouse T-shirts and Mickey Mouse eared hats, they ran around the amusement park acting real "Goofey." They tried to get on every ride in the amusement park, even some of the kiddie rides with their children. They went to Universal Studios and all of the other main attractions. They were even able to hit up the clubs thanks to the 24hr day care facility at the hotel. From sunup to sundown they enjoyed every single second of their week in Disney and it showed because the sun had turned them two shades darker than when they left.

The week in Disney was by far the fastest week they had ever experienced in their lives. Time really does fly by when you're having fun, because when you're not, it seems as if the days are standing still.

Now as they were boarding yet another plane after dropping the kids off, they were leaving again. The pilot came over the intercom and told everybody to buckle up their seatbelts for departure. The sounds of the seatbelts clamping together along with the roar of the Boeing 747 engines as it reached its max for takeoff let everyone know that their journey was about to begin.

Tommy and Mike decided to sit together because from the moment Davita and Ann boarded the aircraft's loading bridge to their first-class seats they hadn't stopped yapping yet. They knew that had they sat with either one of them, they would have never gotten any sleep.

Davita and Ann on the other hand couldn't believe the type of people they were flying with. They were surprised at the passengers walking past them through the first class cabin en-route to the coach cabin in search of their seats. They thought they would be on the plane with a whole bunch of Blacks and foreigners, but they couldn't have been more wrong. The majority of the people on this flight were white. And by the way they were dressed, in Armani and Ferragamo suits, Davita and Ann knew they were people of importance. Even the Black people on the plane with them were dressed like their white counterparts. The only difference was the way they "fashioned" what they wore. The brothas on the plane made the same exact suits the white men wore look totally different, and Davita and Ann took notice.

They loved them some Tommy and Mike, and couldn't see themselves with anybody else, but the brother in seat #2A must've jumped straight out of *GQ* magazine, and they couldn't do anything but stare and admire this God's gift to women. He was black as midnight with pearl-white teeth and eyes. They knew from his high cheekbones and natural looking dreads that he was African. *But damn, he's gorgeous!* they thought and giggled as they peeked back indiscreetly through the narrow space of their own seats in 1A and IB.

The African men on the plane looked nothing like the images flashed across the television screens or the photos plastered inside of *National Geographic* magazine. No flies were on their faces, they didn't look at all like they were dying of malnutrition, and they didn't look one bit uncivilized.

"Damn, how AmeriKKKa lies!" Ann whispered.

"Fuck is so funny?" Tommy asked them, only causing them to laugh harder.

"Nothin'," they answered. "Just enjoying the view, that's all. No harm intended," they finished and chuckled a little more.

Tommy and Mike knew what they were giggling about the moment they saw the brother. He was sharp as hell, they couldn't hate at all, but they damn sure were a little jealous. They knew that their women were just having a little fun, so there was no need to worry. There was nothing wrong with their women enjoying the sight of another good looking man, just as long as that's as far as it went. And the same thing went for them too. There was nothing wrong with *them* enjoying the sight of another good looking sista, just as long as that's as far it went. Those were the rules. By them following this, there was less arguing amongst each other over petty stuff.

When the plane reached its normal altitude the pilot came back over the intercom to inform them that they were allowed to unbuckle their seatbelts. That's when a flight attendant appeared in the middle of the aisle, asking if everyone was alright. Tommy and Mike couldn't help but notice her beauty. They decided right then and there that since their wives wanted to play, they were going to play too. They rang the flight attendant's call button above their heads for her attention.

"May I help you?" The flight attendant stood in their full view and in their personal space and asked them, and instantly

Davita looked right into Tommy's eyes and said, "Why you all up in her face?" under her breath. She said it slow enough for him read her lips, and that made Tommy rub it in even more.

Tommy smiled his playa smile and said, "Yeah, you can help me. Let me get a Bacardi dark, please."

"On the rocks?" she asked.

"No. Straight."

"And you, sir? Would you like anything to drink?" she turned to Mike.

"Yeah, give me the same."

"Okay, so that's two Bacardi darks?" she reconfirmed.

"Yeah," they answered.

"Fine. I'll be right back with your drinks, gentlemen," she said, flashing a beautiful smile while she wrote the orders on a notepad.

When she turned to leave they couldn't believe how long and perfectly shaped her legs, butt and hips were as they stared in admiration. The little stewardess outfit she wore seemed to have been designed by Victoria's Secret the way it revealed so much skin.

"Mmm-mmm-mmm!" they shook their heads and slapped five as she walked away. And that was it!

"Ahn, ahn! Come on, let's go! Give me my seat back! Go over there with your wife," Ann told Tommy.

"For what?" Tommy asked. "We only having a little bit of fun."

"Ahn-huhn! I bet you are. Now give me my seat!" Ann again demanded, and Mike and Tommy laughed as he left her seat.

"Ai'ight cousin," Tommy said going back over to his wife.

"Ai'ight," Mike laughed back.

When the attendant came back with the drinks she noticed the seat changes immediately. The two guys who ordered the drinks were now accompanied by two women. *Must be their wives or girlfriends,* she thought as she approached with the same bright smile she wore when she left.

"Here's your drink, sir. And here's yours, sir," she said, and handed them their drinks.

As she placed the drinks on the trays in front of Tommy and Mike, she felt the angry stares of the two women's eyes glued to her body. The feeling was nothing new to her though. Actually, she had grown accustomed to it. She usually had this effect on other women whenever she was in the presence of them and their mates, even though she showed no interest and was just doing her job.

"Thank you," they replied, and Tommy paid her, tipping her heavily.

"You're welcome, and thank you, sir!" she said, clasping the fifty-dollar bill in her hand.

"Will that be all?"

"For now," Tommy answered.

"Okay then. Just buzz me when you need me," she said, flashing another huge smile, only this one wasn't for Tommy and Mike; it was for Davita and Ann, and they got the message loud and clear.

■■■■■■

The flight to Africa was a fourteen hour flight with three layovers in between. But after sleeping off and on throughout the flight, watching movies that played and a few more drinks, they managed to cut the fourteen hour flight in half. At least that's what it felt like anyway.

Tommy looked over to his wife, Davita as she slept and wondered how she would react when she found out the one and only secret he kept from her. He betrayed her in the worst way and was still going on like he'd done nothing. He wondered if their love was strong enough to withstand what he had done, but he doubted it. Him killing her brother would be unforgivable. That's why he would carry that secret to the grave with him. And even though he knew he had to live with it, the guilt still ate at him whenever he was in his wife's presence. That's why he did so much for her. It was the reason why he went the extra mile to please her. And although he did the majority of special things for her because he wanted too, it still had a way of easing some of the guilt he felt inside for taking her loved one off the face of the earth.

Tommy looked out the window into the clouds and drifted off into another one of his daydreams. The visions that popped up in his head and the memories of what happened in that apartment seven years ago were as clear as the sky he was gazing out into right now...

...Tommy pulled up in front of some row homes down near the Harbor and parked at the curb.

"Right here?" he asked, looking through the rearview mirror at Lil' Shawn in the backseat with Mike.

"Yeah," he nodded his head.

"Nigga, this ain't no apartment complex!" Mike snapped.

"It diz... I thwear it diz!" Lil' Shawn answered toothlessly to the madman at his side. "It'tha house boken down inta two unitz."

"Nigga, I swear to God," Mike said squeezing the words between his clenched teeth, "If you lying..." he said, pausing long enough for his words to sink in, "... I'ma kill you right here!"

"I ain'th lying! Diss ith the spoth. Diss is where ev-ve-ting ith... da money, da drugth... ev-ve-ting! No bulldith, man. I wouldn'th even doe thoo all dith shith if ith wasn'th!" he tried his best to get them to understand and believe him.

"Nigga, shut the fuck up! You ain't got no choice but to go through all this, nigga!"

"I know man. I'm justh sayin'..."

"Saying what, nigga?"

"Nuffin."

"That's what the fuck I thought!" Mike said, and smacked him in the head with the butt of the gun.

"Owww, oooooo!" Lil' Shawn squealed.

"Shut up, nigga!"

Tommy pulled his pre-paid cellphone from the clip and called Hollywood when he was sure this was the right spot, and they sat patiently on his arrival. This particular part of Baltimore was filled with upper to middle class residents, so the street was *rather empty this time of night. It wasn't unusual though, not for a Monday night anyway. They took pride in their over-priced homes and apartments that were listed at prices nearly two to three times their worth because of the location. Had they been built anywhere else, the homes would barely break $110,000, but since the Harbor was in walking distance of the properties, the renters and sellers capitalized off of that, nearly doubling what they spent.*

"Whass good, brother-in-law?" *Hollywood gave him love.*

"Ain't shit. Whass good wit'chu?"

"You know me. You ready for me? Man, I got some fire this time too, you hear me? This shit here could stand at least a seven or eight cut."

"Damn, it's like dat?" *Tommy started figuring numbers in his head.*

"Yeah, it's like dat, lil' brother."

"Same prices?"

"Hell yeah, nigga! For you it's always the same price. Nigga, you family."

"I heard dat. Well look, I'm only a few minutes away from you. I'ma need like ten of them joints... matter fact, gimme fifteen of 'em."

"Ai'ight, nigga. I'll see you when I get here. Are you near?" *Hollywood had to prepare the drop.*

"Coming down 1-95. I'm almost there."

"Ai'ight, well let me make my move then. Hit me when you get to B-More."

"Ai'ight, I'll hit you the." Tommy sighed, knowing what was getting ready to go down.

"What he say?" Skip was ready to get this over.

"He said hit him again when I get to Baltimore. I think he's coming from D.C."

"Ai'ight. Let's wait for a minute then. We'll call 'em back in about 20 minutes. We don't want to call back too soon and that nigga get suspicious on us, feel me?" Skip analyzed.

"Yeah, I feel you. That's what I was going to do anyway." Tommy sat back and waited patiently.

Hollywood pulled in front of the apartment ten minutes after the second call. He parked his Maybach Exelero Coupe Benz across the street from where Tommy, Mike and Skip were unnoticed with a bound Lil' Shawn, and got out of the his car. Like always, Hollywood looked in all directions before crossing the street. Only he wasn't looking for oncoming cars, he was looking for anything irregular that stood out to him -- a person wandering around, a police car -- anything that would send an alarm off inside of him. It was a habit he maintained over the years after reaching the top of the game... a habit he didn't like having because it made him paranoid and he hated it. He hated the fact that he had to walk around everywhere he went and knowing there could be someone following him. He hated the thought that he needed bodyguards everywhere he went. He hated the fact that he didn't know who his enemies were, but he knew that they existed. He knew that they were always right around the corner waiting on him to lunch so they could catch him slippin'. He hated the fact that he knew it was just a matter of time before something bad happened to him. But what he hated the most was that he didn't know the day or the hour when it was going to happen.

Tommy, Skip and Mike watched Hollywood's every move, from the moment he pulled up to now as he crossed the street. When he got out of the car, they noticed that there was someone else in the car with him. There wasn't enough light in the car to actually see who it was, but through the little bit of light, they could see it was a woman. She wasn't their focus though. Their focus was Hollywood and what was hidden in the apartment.

"What about her?" Tommy didn't anticipate a woman to be in the car. Maybe a dude, but not a woman.

"What about her?" Mike didn't give a fuck. "Fuck her! We came for the money and the drugs."

"I'm just sayin', what if she sees us comin' out?" Tommy didn't want anything to go wrong.

"Then we just gonna kill the bitch. Nigga, you know the motto: 'No witnesses left behind'," Mike reminded him. "But like I said, we gonna do this shit so sweet she ain't even gonna know what happened. Loosen up, nigga. You act like you ain't never done this shit be'fo. Nigga, this shit gonna be a cakewalk," Mike finished as Hollywood crossed the street, headed towards the apartment right into the direction of his fate.

The thing he hated the most layed right before him... not knowing when something was going to happen to him. Still searching for anything out of the ordinary, he spotted a black Chevy Celebrity with jet-black tint. Instinct told him to turn around and wait for Tommy to come before going into the apartment, but he ignored the warning signs. His inept sense of pride wouldn't allow him to be scared or uncertain about his move. I need to stop buggin. It's only gonna be a few minutes, he thought, feeling the need to reassure himself. He did that because he felt naked. This was the first time in a long that he was actually by himself without his goons. He was the biggest target alive for the stickup kids, and if they knew he was alone right now, they'd be on him like a pack *of wolves, but he had no real concern he was gonna meet his brothe- in-law. Let me hurry up and do this, he told himself as he walked past the Celebrity, realizing how vulnerable he actually was. He wanted to be all ready when Tommy came to pick up. That way the transaction would be quick and he'd be able to get back to the car with Yolanda.*

Yolanda wasn't his wife or main girl. She was Davita's best friend and his sexual partner. Davita was the one who introduced them years ago, revealing the crush her friend had for him. And since then they'd been fucking. She understood her position in Hollywood's life and shared a mutual agreement. She was at his beck and call whenever he felt the need to fuck, and she was good at it. And for Hollywood's end of the agreement, he was there for her financially at her every begging call. However, that would all come to an end tonight, and for the rest of her life she'd remember one thing... the black Chevy Celebrity.

Hollywood stepped up onto the porch of the row house renovated into two apartments, and fumbled through the keys on his ring until he found the one he was looking for. He placed it into the lock and opened the security door. Then from out of nowhere he began to panic. He felt as though this was where it would all end for him, and sure enough no sooner than he thought it, death in the form of three masked men stepped into the hallway behind him with a bound and beaten Lil' Shawn.

"Nigga, you know what it is!" Skip said. "Where's da mu'fuckin' money?" he continued, and smacked him with the .45 he held in his hand.

The blow caught Hollywood across the bridge of his nose, dropping him to his knees.

"Nigga, where is it!" Mike demanded.

204

But Hollywood didn't respond. He was in total shock. He couldn't believe this was how it would end. He was enraged with himself for not heeding to his premonition. What hurt even more than that was looking into the eyes of Lil' Shawn.

"You bitch-ass nigga!" Hollywood shouted at Lil' Shaw. "You brought these niggas right to me!"

"That's right, Hollywood, your manz. Your right-hand man brought us right here to you. Now if it was me, I would have died before I gave my manz up. But your man right here is a pussy. And you had this nigga wit'chu all the time. I knew he was soft the minute I saw'em," Tommy remarked, and removed his mask. "Yeah nigga, don't look so surprised. It's me, your brother-in-law. Don't worry though, your name is gonna live on and I'ma name my son, the one your sister is carrying right now, after you. That's my gift to you. Now come on, open the door so we can get this money and those drugs. Ain't no need to prolong shit. Both y'all niggaz goin' to die. And you know what's crazy? You goin' to pay for your own funeral," Tommy said before laughing...

...Then he woke up.

The sound of the pilot's voice coming over the speakers of the plane's intercom system was what must have woke Tommy up. "Everyone, please fasten their seatbelts for landing," he said, and Tommy knew their flight to Africa had finally arrived.

Instantly he was overwhelmed with a feeling of joy mixed with anxiety, contentment and pride, which ultimately made him feel relieved. Relieved because he was finally, after all these years of wondering, going to get some answers. Answers to questions he had in his head ever since he was old enough to remember when he was taught who he was. Taught that he was a descendent of African kings and queens. He had these questions locked in his mind because he knew that there was something else more to who he was than what his teachers and history books had told him.

That' why he chose Africa as the vacation spot this time because the questions had plagued him long enough. He was ready to learn the truth.

As soon as they exited the plane, more than two dozen African men and women greeted them. Dressed in traditional garbs and clothing, they wore smiles as big, bright and wide as the Nile River on a beautiful day.

"Hello! Welcome to Africa, our homeland!" the native citizens greeted everyone. "Welcome, brothers and sisters!" they spoke to every Black person that stepped off of the plane.

Damn! Tommy thought, surprised at the warm welcome he just received from the Africans. The way they were welcomed and greeted had totally taken him by surprise. He had prepared himself for the cold shoulder of the Africans because he was taught (well told) that the people of Africa despised and disliked African Americans.

When the small African brother who appeared to be in his late forties in such a nice and friendly way greeted him; he was hesitant. But when he realized it was real and sincere he returned the greeting with a big, bright and wide smile of his own.

Damn, how AmeriKKKa lies! Tommy thought, then looked to Davita, Mike and Ann, who seemed to be just as surprised as he was.

As they made their way from the plane's runway to the actual airport's terminal, their necks were in constant movement. They were taken back by Africa's beauty from the outside looking in. They hadn't even gotten into the city of Africa's Ivory Coast and already noticed the beauty.

"*Oooo*, look, baby!" Davita said excited, pointing over to the huge city off the left of her. "Damn, ain't that pretty!"

"Damn right that's pretty!" Tommy said just as excited to see the huge skyscrapers and tall buildings trimmed in gold -- some with gold domes.

"Damn, I ain't know they had cities in Africa," Mike said bewildered.

"And you wouldn't have known had we not come out to see for ourselves," Ann announced.

"I bet you thought Africa was a big jungle with animals running wild."

"Tell me about it!" Davita agreed.

"Word. They do," Tommy coat tailed off of his wife.

Inside the airport at the luggage claim they were advised by the employees to take company taxis to their hotels or motels instead of independent taxis because many were scam artists. They listened to the advice attentively, and once they got outside in the sweltering heat, they saw taxicabs lined everywhere. So what did they do? They did the exact opposite of what they were told. They took an independent taxi. Tommy was the one who made the decision. He picked out a huge brother driving a white Jeep Wrangler with the top rolled half way back. That in itself had nothing to do with the choice he made. He made the choice because the huge man looked exactly like Uncle Bear.

"Damn, he looks like Uncle Bear!" Tommy said to Mike.

"Damn right he do. That nigga looks like his mu'fuckin' twin," Mike said, not believing his eyes. The man looked like Uncle Bear reincarnated.

"Hello, my brothas and sistas," the huge man spoke humbly before saying, "Thank you for choosing my service. My name is Sunjata." He held out his hand as he offered his greeting.

"Sunjata, it feels as though -- wait, let me rephrase that -- it looks as though like somehow, somewhere, you resemble a relative of mine," Tommy kindly stated. "Here. Look at this." He reached in his back pocket for his wallet. When he dug his wallet out and grabbed his picture of Uncle Bear, he handed it to Sunjata.

Sunjata took the wallet-sized photo and grew wide-eyes as deer caught in headlights. "My God! Who is this man?" Sunjata asked in disbelief.

"That was my Uncle Bear. He's dead now. Murdered by the police," Tommy replied.

"Oh no! I'm sorry to hear that, brotha. Police sometimes are bad, but not all. Some are good. But this man in this picture favors me. Maybe, just maybe we can be kin," Sunjata smiled proudly as he began to neatly load each and every piece of luggage into his jeep. "Where to?" he asked once they were all in his vehicle, and Tommy told him the name of the hotel.

"Novotel Abidjan Hotel on 10th Avenue and Du General De Gaulle."

"Very nice choice, sir! Luxury hotel," Sunjata said nodding.

For the entire ride, all fifteen to twenty minutes of it, Sunjata shared his entire life story to them. They listened eagerly to him go on and on and enjoyed the story. Sunjata told them how he was raised with his two brothers and four sisters, him being the middle child, and how his father had taught him and his brothers to be men -- skilled hunters, fisherman and good workers. He became excited whenever he spoke of his father who was dead now, and

Tommy couldn't remember actually one good thing he'd ever done with his own father. He was like so many other Black boys who grew to be men without a father in their lives.

When he finished his story as he pulled into the hotel, Tommy, Mike, Davita and Ann were thankful. They wanted to hear Sunjata's story but he was over-killing it. They wanted to enjoy the fat of the land, not be told about it the entire trip. They understood his struggle as they hoped the Africans understood the African American struggle as well.

Tommy was the last to get out of the jeep. "How much do we owe you?"

"Seven American dollars," Sunjata answered.

Tommy and Mike both gave him $100.

Sunjata stood there before them with the most modest and humblest look of appreciation on his face. "I'll be here bright and early tomorrow morning," he said, leaving them with a grateful smile on his face. "For your grand tour!"

The next morning, bright and early just like he said, he was at the hotel knocking on their doors.

When Tommy, Davita, Mike and Ann's vacation was finally over and they were back in the United States of AmeriKKKa, they felt renewed in life. However, shortly after that they were reminded of what was really 'hood.

Chapter Twenty-Six

Death Around The Corner

It hadn't even been a complete six months yet and already Zy, Boomer and Peacock had made their mark in the streets as the new top dogs. There wasn't an ounce, four and a half, quarter brick, half of a brick, or a whole brick of cocaine or heroin sold in Delaware from Wilmington to Sussex County that they didn't have in on. It was amazing to them, almost unbelievable the amount of money they saw and drugs they sold in the past months. By the amount of money they made they knew that their bosses, Tommy and Mike had to be millionaires... maybe even double-digit millionaires.

Tommy and Mike, over the years built an empire in the drug game, but why did they hand the reigns over to Zy, Boomer and Peacock like that? That was the question they'd always ask themselves, and the only answer they could come up with was that maybe they were too hot. Maybe they knew it was only a matter of time before they were busted. The other answer was maybe they were just plain tired of the hassle. And a hassle it was. Being on top wasn't as easy as it seemed. There were more than enough problems that came along with the job. There was workers being busted, workers fucking up the money, bail, lawyers... you name it, it happened. So, yes, it was a hassle. In fact, it was a headache, but a headache well worth it. Whatever the case was, the job was theirs now and they loved it.

Tommy and Mike had given them the right-of-way to success, their dream job, and there were only two rules that they had to follow: The first set of rules was that they had to be loyal, honest, hardworking and hungry. The second rule was never to bite the hand that fed them. It was in the "doe boy law book". By doing exactly what they were told to do, the results were instant green --

money green -- money that most dealers never saw. That's when
they realized the importance of a good connect and supreme
clientele, and they had both.

They were enjoying the lifestyle of the rich and famous and
all the luxuries that came along with it, but by doing so they caught
the disease of greed and got arrogant all at the same time. With the
greed and arrogance came severe problems. It caused jealousy
between them, making them envy Tommy and Mike. Most
importantly, it made them break the law, the one that says, "Never
bite the hand that feeds you".

Once they came up in the ranks, other big time dealers
came at them, one Dominican in particular named, José. José
promised them kilos of cocaine at $5,000 apiece and kilos of
heroin at $15,000, and they jumped right on it while still taking
coke and dope from Tommy and Mike. They did that because they
wanted everything to seem the same. They planned on telling
Tommy and Mike later on once their own empire was strong
enough for the war, the war they were sure Tommy and Mike
would start up once they found out. What they didn't know was
that their empire would never reach Tommy and Mike's, and that
their covert move to buy kilos from José was only a part of a plan
greater than theirs; one Tommy and Mike had planned way before
giving them their first package.

When José called Tommy and Mike to tell them about Zy,
Boomer and Peacock's fifth buy, they knew it was time. Time to
put their plan into effect, and it was working out perfectly. Zy,
Boomer and Peacock bit the bait on the hook like a hungry
bigmouth bass in a lake. That's why Tommy and Mike told them
everything, gave them all their clientele and handed the reins of an
empire over to them because they knew in the end their plan would
come together perfectly. They would benefit in more ways than
one. They would get all the drugs they bought from José, they'd
get all their drugs back, plus they'd get all the money Zy, Boomer
and Peacock had all in one swoop. José was just another part of the

plan. In all actuality, he would be their new connect once their stash was gone.

José kept them posted on every move Zy and them made and when they would... and now was the time. Zy, Boomer and Peacock were so blinded by the greed that they never saw it coming. Now as The Hearse made its way to Zy, Boomer and Peacock's stash house, there was a silence in the car that made the air thick.

"Yo, Tommy. You alright cousin?" Mike asked breaking the silence as he drove carefully. He couldn't stand to be pulled over right now because it would take a helluva story to explain why they had duct tape, black garbage bags and two shovels.

"Yeah, I'm alight," Tommy replied. "I'm just thinking about sump'tin', that's all." He could never reveal that he was somewhat remorseful for killing Hollywood. Really he wasn't, but after seeing what distress it caused Davita, sometimes it fucked with his conscience. The visions of that night played over again in his head...

...Hollywood and Lil' Shawn sat bound and gagged in the two kitchen chairs that Skip had placed in the middle of the living room floor while they ransacked the apartment. They moved swiftly but quietly through the place leaving not a spot unsearched.

For the first time in Hollywood's life he was helpless, but engulfed in blind rage. Not like this! he thought as he watched Tommy, Mike and Skip robbed him of everything he worked so hard for. Not like this! Never in a million years would he have thought he'd go out like this but he was and it was happening right now.

His right-hand man, Lil' Shawn had turned on him. He turned his head to look at Lil' Shawn and gave him a look so deadly it could have killed, and Lil' Shawn couldn't return the eye contact. It wasn't that Lil' Shawn was scared or anything like that, it was the fact that he was ashamed. He couldn't muster up enough will to look at Hollywood, especially not after all the killer shit he talked, the killer image he portrayed and the hardcore hit-man shit had been proven to be all an act. Mike had brought his true being to light -- Lil' Shawn was a bitch. Mike had made him give up the tapes. Not only did he lead them to Hollywood, he told them shit they didn't even ask. And now as they were stuffing duffel bags up with kilos of heroin and cocaine he wondered if after all he told they'd at least spare their lives.

"Damn man! Look at this shit!" Tommy yelled from the master bedroom when he found the vault. "Got-damn! This nigga actually got a bank vault in this crib!" Skip said with disbelief. "Yo, Mike! Go get that nigga Hollywood and make that nigga open up this fuckin' door!"

Mike snatched Hollywood up out of the chair by his shoulders and forced him to the bedroom. The thought of taking a bullet to the head instead of opening the safe sounded good, but there was still that little piece of optimism left in Hollywood's head that told him to go against it... go against it because there was still a chance that they'd let them live to see another day. So as he stood before the huge steel door he opened it up. Hollywood stepped aside and watched as they walked into his vault. This was where his entire kitty was stashed. Everything that he had worth some importance was in here. Naked pictures of his wifey, guns, car titles, deeds to homes he owned, jewelry and most of all, every dollar he had. He had the vault built especially for that. He figured that there was no way in the world that he could possibly deposit this amount of money in a bank, so he built his own.

Tommy, Mike and Skip stuffed valuables in pillowcases, whatever they could take out of there. Cautiously, they placed the goods in the car searching to see if the girl was still present; she wasn't. Hollywood would never see the note Yolanda left telling him that she walked to the Harbor to grab a bite to eat at Phillips Seaford Restaurant, since he was talking so long.

After they finished taking things down to The Hearse, Tommy, Mike and Skip headed back to finish the job. Tommy led the way, while Mike tail ended the two into the apartment, carrying a tin can of gasoline.

Tommy walked over to Hollywood and Lil' Shawn and towered over them as they looked up from the chairs in defeat. "Why the long face, niggas? Ain't no need for that shit now. It's over" Tommy had no sympathy. "Yo, Skip, how my boy, Sha-Rock used to say it?"

"'Caught you slippin', nigga!'," Skip and Mike said in unison.

"Dat's right, niggaz, caught you slippin'," Tommy repeated and snatched the tape from their mouths.

Hollywood looked at Tommy in disgust. The nerve of this ungrateful-ass nigga! he thought, cursing himself for being so stupid. He made it a rule to never let anyone get too close to him, but with Tommy it was different. This was his sister's husband and a friend to him. He should have at least known to give himself more time to know Tommy. Especially since the nigga had a name for himself in the streets and one that carried respect at that. Anyone who could do that had to be about his work. And now as Hollywood sat defenseless, he cursed himself again. Damn!

"Whass wrong, nigga? What? You ain't got nuffin' to say?" Tommy chastised. "Well, I do. Yo, check this out. Hollywood you's a good nigga but for the dough... you got to go! Fuck it. Look at it this way; You done more shit in your lifetime than most niggas ever did. Plus nigga, your name is going to live on. Now, tell me that ain't good lookin' out. Yo, Mike, I'm done wit' these *niggaz. Come handle your bizness,"* Tommy *cued, and* Mike *doused them in gasoline.*

"Here you go, cousin," Tommy said and tossed Hollywood a blunt. "That's good haze too, nigga. Go 'head and celebrate. Yo, Mike, give 'im a light," Tommy finished, and Mike tossed a match on the top of them.

Their screams as they went up could've been heard on death ears. But to Tommy, Mike and Skip, they were mute. They left the apartment as it went up in flames. The only thing that Yolanda would remember about the last time she saw Hollywood would be that black Chevy Celebrity. It would be etched in her brain forever.

When Tommy and Mike pulled up to Zy, Boomer and Peacock's stash house, the first part of their plan was done. They were there. They parked the Celebrity a block away from the house and crept on the porch silently.

From day one, the first day they put Zy, Boomer and Peacock on, they waited for this moment. The moment to prove these "*loyal, I'm down wit' you Tommy and Mike*" niggas wrong. All that talk was a bunch of bullshit. Especially, when it came to the game. Filled with adrenaline, Tommy and Mike held their guns n their sides and knocked on the door.

■■■■■■

Inside the house Zy, Boomer and Peacock were counting their money for the third and final time. They knew that if Tommy and Mike knew that not only were they pumping for them, but also buying their own on the side, they'd take it as a direct insult. That's why they kept it under the wrap. What they didn't know was that Mike and Tommy had already known of their young boys' betrayal since the first time they brought something from José.

215

"Yo, go get the door, Boomer. Tell them niggaz ain't nothin' right now. We gonna open up shop later on," Zy said.

"Ai'ight," Boomer said and got up to get the door. "Who is it?" he asked and looked through the peephole.

"It's me, nigga!" Tommy said.

"Oh shit! Whass'up y'all?" Boomer said as he opened the door cautiously.

"Whass good wit' y'all?" Tommy asked, sliding the gun back down into his waistline.

"Ain't shit. Just chillin', that's all."

"I heard that!" Tommy responded as they entered the house.

Boomer led Tommy and Mike in to the kitchen where Zy and Peacock sat at the table in front of piles of money and they all spoke. "Whass'up?"

"Hey, whass good, niggas?"

"Y'all is whass good. I see y'all eatin' now. I told y'all, y'all was on the winning team," Tommy said, and they agreed.

"You wasn't lying," Peacock said, and never saw it coming. None of them did. In a flash, right before their eyes, Tommy and Mike had them at gunpoint. Their movements were so swift that none of them -- Zy, Boomer or Peacock -- could react.

"Don't even think about it, lil' niggas and don't look so surprised. It's over. I told you never bite the hand that feeds you. But no, y'all niggas had to try y'alls hand!"

"What 'chu talkin' 'bout?" they asked dumbfounded and scared to death.

"Nigga, you know what I'm talking about!" Mike snapped and smacked Zy with the butt of the gun. "Stop insultin' my intelligence."

"For real man, I don't know what you talkin' about!"

"Nigga, I'm talkin' about José! The nigga you buying that coke from!" Tommy yelled, and they were speechless. They looked at each other like, *Daaammmn! How they know that?* but also knew they were busted.

Each one of them was trying to think of a way out of what their greed had cost them, and Zy blurted out, "Tommy, maaaan, it ain't even like that. We were just try'na flip our money, that's all."

"Nigga, you could have done that wit' us," Tommy said.

"I don't give a fuck! Y'all don't do no shit like dat! Y'all should've waited," Mike said, and smacked Peacock with the pistol knocking him out of the chair.

When Peacock hit the floor he clutched his head with both hands trying to shake the cobwebs. And he knew just by the way Tommy and Mike were looking that they weren't here for any games. Which meant if they couldn't figure a way out of this house, this would probably be the last day of their lives. Peacock looked to Zy and Boomer and noticed just through their eyes that they were thinking the same thing, and the feeling was nearly indescribable. Unless you have been put in a position where you were staring down the barrel of a gun totally submissive to the man or men on the other side of that handle, you can't relate. They could. They saw death around the corner.

"Get da fuck up, nigga! I'm tired of looking at ya punk ass on the brink of tears... all you niggaz!" Mike punked them. "Looking at all this punk shit y'all displaying makes me wanna kill y'all bitch asses *now!*"

"Hold up, Mike, not yet. Not until these mu'fuckas help us fill up these bags with this coke, dope and this money." Tommy was making them work one last time. "Now come on lil' niggaz; get to work. Fill them bags up."

And instantly they followed their directive.

"Oh... and don't forget the floor, nigga," Tommy added, knowing about the secret compartment in the kitchen floor -- the one he had advised them to get from the same man who did theirs at Kelly's house. But unlike the one Tommy and Mike had in the basement, theirs was built in the kitchen.

As soon as all the money and drugs were placed in the duffel bags that Tommy and Mike tossed them, Peacock headed for the light switch on the wall. And just like at Kelly's house, Peacock removed the light switch casing from the wall and reached inside for the switch. Like magic the hydraulic system came to life and the kitchen floor began to open up. When it stopped, to Tommy and Mike's surprise, the entire compartment was nearly filled to the top with neatly stacked money and a pile of bricks wrapped in duct tape and wax paper.

"Jackpot, niggaz! Jackpot!" Tommy said to Mike, who flashed a smile.

"Dat too, niggas. Don't stand there like you don't know the routine," Mike said, and watched as they continued to work. "Yo, Tommy, watch these niggaz while I go out to load the car," Mike directed, tossing duffel bags over his shoulders and carrying the remaining in his hands.

"Ai'ight, go ahead, my nigga."

"You gonna be ai'ight?" Mike joked, looking at the three sets of fearful eyes.

"Do bears shit in the woods?"

"I know dat's right!" Mike replied, and they shared a laugh with one another that was hardly funny to Zy, Boomer and Peacock.

By the time Mike returned from the car, the three of them, Zy, Boomer and Peacock, had totally emptied the compartment. Now there was only one thing remaining to do; Finish the job.

Tommy and Mike ordered them to stand in front of the empty compartment one by one. And then raised their guns with the silencers on the barrel and took target practice.

The first to go was Peacock. *"Sneep! Sneep!"* The guns sounded, silencing to them to a minimum but not taking away the power, as the bullets -- one to the head, the other to the chest -- sent Peacock flying from his feet backwards into his new resting place. The same went for Zy. But for Boomer it went a little different. Before his execution-style murder and final resting place, he smiled, told them to kiss his ass, then spit into their direction. The bullets riddled him. Instead of only two, they emptied their clips.

When it was all over, Tommy hit the switch, replaced the casing, and he and Mike left just as smoothly and quietly as they came.

"You know what, Tommy?" Mike asked as they walked to the car.

"What's that, cousin?"

"When somebody else moves into that same house, them niggaz goin' to still be there."

"Fuck 'em!" Tommy said. "I ain't gonna lose no sleep, are you?"

"Imagine dat!" and The Hearse drove smoothly away.

To their surprise, they didn't have to use the duct tape, black garbage bags or shovels.

Chapter Twenty-Seven

Life's a Bitch

The news of Zy, Boomer and Peacock's disappearance spread throughout the city like the H.I.V. virus spread amongst homosexuals, heterosexuals and needle users. The lead detectives were Detective Gamble, who was promoted years ago for his outstanding work ethics, and his new partner, a veteran, Detective Cohen.

Cohen was puzzled almost spooked at the similarities of this case and the one he came across before -- a slew of them to be exact -- ones that were nearly perfectly executed like this one.

As Detective Gamble poured his fourth cup of coffee, he thought back to the day he ended Bearacus Good's life. Instead of being reprimanded, he was commended. It felt good though; he took a dangerous man off the streets and was rewarded for it. Now, he sat with his partner, a long time veteran on the police force with a gravy job, until this.

Detective Cohen thought back to the house as he drank a cup of coffee with Gamble. He came to the conclusion that that had to be the crime scene, even though they had yet to make it official. He knew for sure it had to be because each one of their cars was parked right out front and neighbors said they saw them enter the house together. The funny thing was that no one saw them leave. He also determined this was the crime scene because the evidence collector found speckles of blood splattered through the kitchen.

"*Damn!*" he shouted in his dark and empty office lit only by the lamp on his desk, as he slammed down his cup of coffee. "*Damn!*" he shouted again. Frustration was beginning to win the battle over him. It was frustrating because it was as if Rasul, Dog, Pretty E and Hit-man were back to claim their positions in the streets as bosses, but he knew that wasn't the case. He knew that because after all these years, he kept them under a close microscope. His reason for doing so was because somewhere deep down inside of him, he knew. He knew they were responsible for the death of his partner and mentor, Detective Armstrong, and his new partner, Detective Gamble had no idea what vengeance he had for the four Black men. Gamble had his own set of issues.

Cohen looked towards the ceiling and said aloud as if he was talking directly to his old partner, "I'm beginning to see why you crossed over, ole buddy. I really am," he said, referring to why Armstrong became crooked. "There's just too much work to do for this little amount of pay. Hell, I can barely put my kids through college. Think of how we put our lives on the line every day for a little over $47,000 a year. Then, to top that off, the same criminals we chase down and arrest are protected by Constitutional Rights. I swear!" Detective Cohen began shaking his head. "If I don't crack this case wide open, I'm going to either retire or cross-over like you did, partner."

With that, he stood from behind his desk and informed Detective Gamble he was on his way home. "Gamble, hit the lights would you on your way out."

"Sure, Cohen. See you in the morning." Gamble continued to fill out his case report.

Chapter Twenty-Eight

It's a Dirty Game

Tommy and Mike moved along with their lives just as normal as they had in the past. They were satisfied with the job, and by the way the media talked, they knew the police were totally at a dead end road. The only thing bad about the three disappearances was that the police had the city under siege. From sun up to sun down police were on every corner in the city. It was impossible for anyone to make money illegally on the streets. For Tommy and Mike, that wasn't a problem. They were continuously making money thanks to Marcus. Even though they didn't have to sell drugs, when they weren't, things didn't seem normal. Uncle Bear handed them to the game and they both signed "Hood Lifetime Contracts". Forever, they would play the game.

Tommy drove through the city in The Hearse and watched as the eyes of every single person who saw it revealed the look of fear. Mostly everyone in the underground world knew the affiliation between Tommy, Mike and the three missing boys. No one inquired about them for one simple fact they didn't want to be next. However, they did wonder what they had done to Tommy Good and Mike. Did they fuck up some money? Were Tommy and Mike just plain tired of them? Many questions came to their minds' but went no further than that.

Tommy cruised down 3rd Street like he always did, coasting. He saw the same two young boys with that look in their eyes sitting on the corner in the same spot he'd seen them day after day. Even though he never met them, he was familiar with them from the nods they gave each time he rode through. Although these young boys not only had the look of hunger, they had the eyes of tigers desperate for a meal.

"Whass'up, youngin's?" Tommy called out to them. "What y'all up to?"

"Nuffin, *papi*," the Spanish one of the two responded. "You know, just doin' what we do, feel me?" They knew exactly who Tommy Good was and prayed that he wanted to put them down.

"I feel you." Tommy smiled. "But what actually is it y'all do?"

"We tryin' to pump this diesel. You know this is the only real dope spot in Wilmington besides Riverside and the Eastside," the other one spoke up, sounding more Dominican than his actual Black heritage.

"Whass'up then? Y'all tryin' to get some real paper?" Just like Zy, Boomer and Peacock they lit up at the opportunity to get on Tommy Good's team.

"Damn right!" they answered together.

"Take a ride with me." Tommy unlocked the door and let them in. The ride they took that day was the same ride the other youngin's took when they were first hired on the team, but opposite of them. These two tigers had bigger plans.

When the ride was over and Tommy took them back to 3rd Street. They knew they were about to blow up. The only difference was they weren't going out like Zy, Boomer or Peacock. They wouldn't be the ones to come up missing.

■■■■■■

Tommy pulled in front of Big Mom's house for a brief visit. Her house was still the meeting house for the family when they wanted to visit.

"Big Mom, you alright?" Tommy hollered as he heard the pots and pans dropping loudly to the floor.

Just like his younger years, Big Mom was always aiming to please, that's why she was in the kitchen. In the event someone stopped over, she had to have a pot of something brewing.

"Aw, Tommy, I'm fine. A couple of pots fell thats all," she paused. "I'm so glad you came to visit. Since y'all don' got all grown hardly nobody comes at the same time. You know I didn't raise y'all to be this way. We were a family! Family sticks together. The only one sticking 'round here is that damn Willie. His ass won't go anywhere. The rest of them rarely come 'round and when they do, like I said, ain't nobody else 'round. Not you, Tommy. You always come to check on Big Mom."

"I know that's right, baby!"

"It would be nice if you got all the family together like old times. A family reunion would be real nice and it's past due. You know I ain't getting' no younger. I want to see my great-grands before my time comes, Tommy."

"Yeah, that'll work. I'll pull this thing together for you, baby."

"You know Bear would be proud. You stepped up as a man and took on his role."

"How 'bout that. I loved my uncle to death."

"Th-The-Then--" Big Mom stuttered a bit, "--Why is Gamble still living?"

Tommy was stuck. He didn't know how to respond. Gamble was still living and his uncle was dead. Was Big Mom talking out of hurt or was she giving him the cue to off a man?

Tommy didn't know what to think. The only thing he could think of was Big Mom wanted Gamble dead.

"Don't say another word, Big Mom. It's handled."

Big Mom smiled at him and then reminded him, "Now, don't forget about your mother. She may be H.I.V. positive and still on drugs, but she is your mother. Make sure Candice get invited like Rhonda and Robin. Go on over to the church and tell Mia I want her to come too. You know she found the Lord when Bear died."

"Yeah, I know but you think she's still in church? That was years ago."

"But a lifetime of pain!" She leaned on the center nook in her kitchen and wiped her face with a cloth. "I'm sure she's still standing if I am."

"I heard that!" Tommy walked over and gave her a tight squeeze. He wondered if Davita would feel this way if she ever found out the truth about her brother's death. *A lifetime of pain*. He was sure this would damage his relationship with his wife.

I'll do what I can, Big Mom. It may take sometime though but I'll get it together. Just like old times for ya, baby!"

Big Mom smiled and gave him one last hug. "Come back later for some good ole soul food, baby, you hear me?"

"I will." Tommy left with other things on his mind.

He left Big Mom's en-route to his house. When he pulled up in his driveway, he instantly became agitated because he wanted to get some rest. However, the plates on the Honda parked in his spot had DC tags on it, so he knew Yolanda and Shaylynn were visiting. He wasn't for all that "girl talk" this time and was pissed when he entered his house.

"Hey, Tommy!" they spoke, happy to see him, but switched up when he didn't greet them back.

"Oh, you bein' smart now?" Shaylynn sucked her teeth.

"Tommy, don't be so ignorant." Davita went over and kissed her husband on one of his thick arms.

"I'm not. I just wanted some peace and quiet. With these two loud ass mouths in the house, I know that's not possible."

"Ain't nobody thinking 'bout Tommy, Vita, but you!" Yolanda said as he walked up the stairs to his bedroom.

"Fuck you, Yolanda! You a bad influence on my wife anyway!"

"Whatever! Davita girl, we 'bout to bounce."

"Tommy must be on his period," Shaylynn joked.

"I'll be glad when both of y'all leave!" He turned back around before making it to the top step.

"What the fuck is wrong wit' him? Girl, I don't see how you put up with him. You don't have to. You got your own money and two practices. Leave dat nigga!"

"For what? 'Cause he trippin' today? Girl, he ain't like that all the time. My baby must be stressed or something for him to act like that. You know he sometimey anyway," Davita defended him.

"I know that's right!" Shaylynn agreed.

Davita stood up from the couch and showed her friends to the door, but when Yolanda stepped outside she froze dead in her tracks. At first she tried to deny it, but how could she? There was no doubt in her mind; that was it! The vehicle she saw speeding away from the apartment the night of Hollywood's murder. Her heart nearly stopped from the shock and her knees shook uncontrollably to the point she could barely stand. Instantly, she was overwhelmed with emotion and the tears started falling from her eyes.

Oh my fuckin' God! she thought at the idea that Tommy played a part in Hollywood' murder. She turned to face Davita and Shaylynn and thought, *Damn! How am I going to tell my girl this shit?* She thought about not saying anything fearing for her life, but with the tears that were streaming down her face how could she lie and say that nothing was wrong? *What am I going to do?* she pleaded with her emotions. Her first thought was not to tell her anything, but that wouldn't be right. Davita deserved to know who was responsible for the murder of her brother, even if it was at the hands of her husband.

"What's wrong, Yolanda?" Davita and Shaylynn consoled her.

"Nuffin'," she hesitated before blurting out, "Davita, that's the vehicle!"

"What vehicle?" Davita asked, lost.

"The vehicle that sped away from the apartment complex your brother was in right before it went up in flames."

"What!?"

Davita was speechless.

"That's it! That's it!" Yolanda repeated, crying.

Davita tried with everything she had in her not to believe what Yolanda confessed out of her mouth, but she knew her husband's M.O. and she knew Tommy and Mike drove The Hearse when they were on capers, but a caper against her brother, she just couldn't imagine. The pain she felt just thinking that her husband played a serious role: at the funeral, to her mom, at the house, to their kids. The thought that he would do something like this was overbearing. It felt as though someone literally reached in her chest and squeezed her heart into a clenched fist. The hurt that showed on Davita's face as the truth of what her husband conspired in made Yolanda and Shaylynn concerned for her life. She almost looked faint. Then as if she was possessed, her hurt turned to anger.

"Shaylynn, take my kids to my mom's. They are at the park. Scoop them up and don't turn back. I'll be alright. Just take them to my mom's, *now!*"

"You ain't about to do nuffin' crazy are you?" Yolanda asked as they walked down the walkway.

Davita smirked. "Nah, girl, I ain't that stupid. I'll tell you this though; this marriage is over! Y'all call me when you get to D.C. okay?" she said and closed the door.

She stood staring out the window until she was sure they had pulled off. With tears of anger welled up in her eyes, she walked into the den and over to the bookcase where her 9mm Ruger sat on the bookshelf. She slowly pulled out the books, *Blinded, Block Party* and *Harlem Girl Lost*, and there it sat, fully loaded. With trembling hands, she grabbed the gun and headed upstairs to where her Tommy was laying in the bed and crept into the room.

"You Muthafuckin' Bastard!" Davita screamed at the top of her lungs. *"You killed my brother!"*

"Wait, baby, wait!" Tommy sat up in the bed. Good thing he hadn't fallen asleep.

"Yolanda told me she seen The Hearse. It was you all along! You even begged me to name our son after him and you took his life! How could you? How could you do this to me, Tommy? Why did you do this? You threw it all away. I loved you! How could you?" The tears and sweat poured down Davita's face. No matter how much her life changed, she could look past other situations, but this was the ultimate betrayal. She couldn't look past this.

In a rage, Tommy jumped from the bed. He thought about trying to talk his way out of this, but decided against it. Davita was too far gone. He had a better chance of trying to strip her of the gun. So on that, he jumped out bed and dove straight at her.

"Pow!" The gun sounded.

Both of them dropped to the floor. Davita's eyes were stuck and so were Tommy's. He didn't feel any heat, but he saw the blood on his wifebeater. He closed his eyes and opened them slowly, peering down at the Ruger. He didn't know how, but his fingers were on the trigger. He wasn't shot -- Davita was. Tommy's head went back as Davita's eyes stayed stuck. He panicked. He didn't know which move to make so he ran out leaving his wife for dead.

■■■■■

Davita's body lay motionless on the bedroom floor. Blood trickled from her chest, her eyes still staring. She knew that for her to survive she had to play dead, and knew she didn't have much time before she bled to death. Her eyes blinked as she gradually reached for the end of the bed to get up.

"You don' fucked up now, Tommy Good!" She pressed tightly on her gunshot wound. "This ain't over mothafucka!"

Street Knowledge!
"So Real You Think You've Lived It!"

Note From The Author:

Note From The Author: This is a Surah from the Holy Koran, and Hadith narrated by Abu Hurairah., that we all need to take heed to.

Surah 49:12 "Koran"
    O you who believe! Avoid much suspicion indeed. Some suspicions are sins... And spy not, neither backbite one another. Would one of you like to eat the flesh of his dead brother? You would hate it (so hate backbiting). And fear Allah (God). Verily, Allah is the One who forgives and accepts repentance, Most Merciful.

Hadith: Narrated by Abu Hurairah (R.A.A.)
Allah's Messenger (P.B.U.H.) said;

    "Beware of suspicion, for suspicion is the worst of false tales; and do not look for other's faults, And do not do spying on one another, And do not practice Najsh* And do not be jealous of one another, And do not hate one another, And do not desert (stop talking to) one another... And O Allah's worshippers! (God's worshipper's) Be Brothers!"

*Najsh – to offer a high price for something in order to allure another customer who is interested in a thing.

Other Novels

By

Leondrei Prince

Bloody Money
Me & My Girls
Bloody Money 2
Bloody Money III City Underseige

...Coming Soon...

The Rise & Fall of The Capelli Family
And
Frankie 'Lil' Frankie' Maraachi, III

The Tommy Good Story Part II

Upcoming Novels From
Street Knowledge Publishing

..Coming 2008..

Dipped Up
By: Visa Rollack

No Love-No Pain
By: Sicily

Lust, Love, & Lies
By: Eric Fleming

The Fold
By: Tehuti Atum-Ra

Dopesick 2
By: Sicily

Court In The Streets 2
By: Kevin Bullock

Pain Freak
By: Gregory Garrett

NEMESIS
By: Tehuti Atum-Ra

Stackin' Paper
By: JoeJoe

Shakers
By: Gregory D. Dixon

A Day After Forever 2
By: Willie Dutch

Unlovable Bitch By:
Allysha Hamber

Street Knowledge Publishing Order Form

Street Knowledge Publishing, P.O. Box 345, Wilmington, DE 19801
Email: jj@streetknowledgepublishing.com
Website: www.streetknowledgepublishing.com

For Inmates Orders and Manuscript Submissions
P.O. Box 310367, Jamaica, NY 11431

Bloody Money
ISBN # 0-9746199-0-6 $15.00
Shipping/ Handling Via
U.S. Priority Mail $5.25
Total $20.25

Me & My Girls
ISBN # 0-9746199-1-4 $15.00
Shipping/ Handling Via
U.S. Priority Mail $5.25
Total $20.25

Bloody Money 2
ISBN # 0-9746199-2-2 $15.00
Shipping/ Handling Via
U.S. Priority Mail $5.25
Total $20.25

Dopesick
ISBN # 0-9746199-4-9 $15.00
Shipping/ Handling Via
U.S. Priority Mail $5.25
Total $20.25

Money-Grip
ISBN # 0-9746199-3-0 $15.00
Shipping/ Handling Via
U.S. Priority Mail $5.25
Total $20.25

The Queen of New York
ISBN # 0-9746199-7-3 $15.00
Shipping/ Handling Via
U.S. Priority Mail $5.25
Total $20.25

Don't Mix The Bitter With The Sweet
ISBN # 0-9746199-6-5 $15.00
Shipping/ Handling Via
U.S. Priority Mail $5.25
Total $20.25

Street Knowledge Publishing, P.O. Box 345, Wilmington, DE 19801
Email: jj@streetknowledgepublishing.com
Website: www.streetknowledgepublishing.com

The Hunger
ISBN # 0-9746199-5-7   **$15.00**
Shipping/ Handling Via
U.S. Priority Mail   **$5.25**
Total   **$20.25**

Sin 4 Life
ISBN # 0-9746199-8-1   **$15.00**
Shipping/ Handling Via
U.S. Priority Mail   **$5.25**
Total   **$20.25**

The Tommy Good Story
ISBN # 0-9799556-0-2   **$15.00**
Shipping/ Handling Via
U.S. Priority Mail   **$5.25**
Total   **$20.25**

The NorthSide Clit
ISBN # 0-9746199-9-X   **$15.00**
Shipping/ Handling Via
U.S. Priority Mail   **$5.25**
Total   **$20.25**

Bloody Money III
ISBN # 0-9799556-4-5   **$15.00**
Shipping/ Handling Via
U.S. Priority Mail   **$5.25**
Total   **$20.25**

Court in the Streets
ISBN # 0-9799556-2-9   **$15.00**
Shipping/ Handling Via
U.S. Priority Mail   **$5.25**
Total   **$20.25**

A Day After Forever
ISBN # 0-9799556-1-0   **$15.00**
Shipping/ Handling Via
U.S. Priority Mail   **$5.25**
Total   **$20.25**

Street Knowledge Publishing, P.O. Box 345, Wilmington, DE 19801
Email: jj@streetknowledgepublishing.com
Website: www.streetknowledgepublishing.com

Dipped Up
ISBN # 0-9799556-5-3   **$15.00**
Shipping/ Handling Via
U.S. Priority Mail   **$5.25**
Total   **$20.25**

Playn' for Keeps
ISBN # 0-9799556-9-6   **$15.00**
Shipping/ Handling Via
U.S. Priority Mail   **$5.25**
Total   **$20.25**

Stackin' Paper
ISBN # 0-9755811-1-2   **$15.00**
Shipping/ Handling Via
U.S. Priority Mail   **$5.25**
Total   **$20.25**

Street Knowledge Publishing LLC
Purchaser Order Form

Date: _____

Purchaser _____

Mailing Address _____

City _____ State _____ Zip Code_____

Quantity	Title of Book	Price Each	Total
	Bloody Money	$ 15.00	$
	Bloody Money 2	15.00	
	Me & My Girls	15.00	
	Dopesick	15.00	
	Money-Grip	15.00	
	The Queen Of New York	15.00	
	Don't Mix The Bitter With The Sweet	15.00	
	Sin 4 Life	15.00	
	The NorthSide Clit	15.00	
	The Hunger	15.00	
	The Tommy Good Story	15.00	
	Court In The Streets	15.00	
	Bloody Money III	15.00	
	Playin' For Keeps	15.00	
	A Day After Forever	15.00	
	No Love, No Pain	15.00	
	Dipped-Up	15.00	
	Lust, Love & Lies	15.00	
	Total Books Ordered	Subtotal	
		Shipping	
	(Priority Mail $5.25 each) (If ordering more than one add $2.00 each)		
		Total	$